# THE ROOT WORKER

# THE ROOT WORKER

## RAINELLE BURTON

THE OVERLOOK PRESS
WOODSTOCK & NEW YORK

First published in the United States in 2001 by
The Overlook Press, Peter Mayer Publishers, Inc.
Woodstock & New York

WOODSTOCK:
One Overlook Drive
Woodstock, NY 12498

NEW YORK:
386 West Broadway
New York, NY 10012

*Typeformatting by Bernard Schleifer Company*
Manufactured in the United States of America

ISBN 1-58567-140-1

*To my children,*

*Tiran and Raymond,*

*who have always had a habit of bringing the world to me.*

*And to the world.*

*I'm here. Yes.*

# THE ROOT WORKER

# PROLOGUE

KNOW WHAT, CLARISSA?

I tried to figure out what went wrong this time. Sometimes I see where it's our fault but other times I just don't know what happens—why you stay so sad all the time.

The Woman said God doesn't love ugly. Always said that. Well if that's the case He must really be through with you, ugly as you are. Just kidding, Clarissa. I'm trying to make you laugh. But you're never in much of a laughing mood.

It's okay to be ugly, I like you anyway. But I don't know if it's okay to joke about God, He might strike you down. I haven't been struck down yet but you sure have.

I don't know if I really believe in God. It's a sin not to believe in Him, I know. I do believe in sin. And heaven and hell too. But I don't know if I believe in God. Sometimes I believe and other times I don't. When I don't I won't admit it. I don't want to go to hell and I don't want God to strike me down.

Know what else, Clarissa?

Sometimes you lie too, I know. The Woman said that a child who lies will kill her own mother. Maybe that's why it happens.

But you don't lie all the time, only when you're in trouble. Most of the time you don't say anything at all—just sit there like you're doing now looking sad and ugly.

You need to have a soul so you can pray. They say that God steps in and saves you when you do. I don't know about that either. The martyrs prayed and they were killed.

What you really need is to get to Glue. You can't get there if they get you first though. You never know when they're going to get you it happens so fast. But I do. I can tell just like I can smell the rain before it storms.

# WOMANHOOD

I HELPED MARCUS LOOK FOR WORMS UNDER THE BACKPORCH steps. When it rains, the worms come up from under the dirt. That's what it did last night so we caught a lot this morning.

I pried the corner of the tin sign from the house. A chunk of wood held to its rusty edge on a nail that should have come out of the house but took a piece of it instead.

Last year the Husband said he would paint the sign, Clarissa. That was when he found it down the alley and the Woman had a fit. Need it to keep the rain out from under the steps he told her, said the wood's getting soft. He called it a little pliant. The Woman called it rot. "Always patching rot," she said. "Windows, toilet, roof, now this. Patch and chink. But it don't do no good cause it's an old rotting piece of shit."

The Husband said the foundation's strong so that ought to count for some worth.

He painted part of the sign but stopped when he saw the new green was too bright for the old yellow-green of the house. Now the sign says WITH UPTOWN SODA POP in faded orange letters. The paint spot covers the LIVE IT UP part.

Marcus leaned the sign against the house and we crawled into the hole to dig in the mud. We filled up one can with worms and started on another one but the Woman came home and I had to stop.

Marcus said we caught enough to probably make a dollar fifty if he can take them to Belle Isle and sell them to some grownups who fish there. If he sells them to some boys he'll make about fifty cents.

The Woman said I can't be around him for the next few days because I have the Curse. I don't know much about it except I started to bleed all of a sudden for no reason at all and it's been three or four days now and never stopped. I don't know if it ever will. But it doesn't hurt so I just forget about it sometimes. I know I can't touch the flowers while I have it, it would make them die. The Woman told me that. Can't touch Marcus either she said. Something awful could happen to him if I did and she'd kill me for it. And there's the womanhood rags I have to burn as soon as I take them off. Someone could use them to do things to her.

I don't know why they're called *womanhood* rags. It seems like it would mean they're for a woman. I'm not a woman, I know. Eleven and a half is too young to be one and I don't look like one, act like one, or feel like one. But she said I am a woman now, said "I don't know how this house is gonna stand having *two* women in it" as soon as she found out I started bleeding.

I still don't know much about what this has to do with being around Marcus except it must have something to do with the reason why his teeth are crooked. The Woman told Aunt Della she didn't understand why here in Detroit they let girls go to school and be around boys when they have the Curse.

"Can mess a boy up," she said. "Back where I come from, in my time they didn't have none of that. A girl had the Curse she was put up someplace where she couldn't get near nobody till it was all over with. Folks could get messed up and they knew it."

I'm glad we're not back where she came from. I don't want to miss school and I'd miss Marcus. I like him almost as much as I like you, Clarissa. When the Woman leaves I sneak and play with him. I try hard not to touch him though, don't want anything bad to happen.

Yesterday we made a game out of it. I was It because I have the womanhood rag. The alley fence was Glue. Marcus didn't want it to be, said James caught his elbow on its rusty wire. But there's nothing for Glue near the side fences. Just muddy dirt near the one between our house and the old people's, sand near the other one. But weeds are near the alley fence. Weeds tall as our knees. Some grow through the wire that's not bent.

I like the alley fence. There I can see every house on the other street. Every porch—some still good, others patched with siding, tin, wood. All the yards—two with grass and flowers, others full of weeds. The rest just sand and dirt naked. I watch the people who live in them go about their business. Sometimes they shake their heads at the patches, the weeds, the nakedness. Sometimes they don't notice at all.

Got an A on the Catechism test.

Marcus hates Catechism. But when Sister talks about God and the saints and all the stuff about heaven and archangels, it seems like she's telling us stories about places that are secret and people who are invisible. It's like being in a dream I don't want to wake up from. I let my ears hold on to every word she says while I close my eyes and look inside my head to see all the people doing secret invisible things.

I imagine them—even God—until they become real, but nobody can see them but me. It's like magic or something. It seems like it might be a sin to say that God's like magic so I don't say anything about what He's like. I just listen and imagine. Sister said that nobody can remember as much in Catechism as I can.

I imagine souls in purgatory. Souls, not people. All kinds. Babies who died before they could get baptized, grownups and kids who died with sins that weren't mortal—which would take them straight to hell—but venial that would take them to the middle. Venial sin souls, stuck between visible and invisible, looking like pieces of fog floating around between heaven and hell. Scared and screaming because they can feel at least some of hell's fire. Not all of it—only people in hell can feel *all* of the fire. They burn and scream, Clarissa, for hundreds of years. But not for eternity. Or until someone saves them with indulgences. Indulgences are like Glue from all the suffering.

When Sister talks about hell I think about root working. A lot of it. I imagine people down deep under the bottom of the ground working roots all the time, stealing rags and drawers and hair and everything else from each other. I imagine them putting down powder all the time, burning stuff all the time. That's why there's so much fire. And I see the Root Worker laughing at the devil because he keeps trying to make her burn but can't—she's as powerful as he is—while all the other people down there spend the rest of eternity burning and scared of both of them.

We're going to heaven, Clarissa.

We took the long way home this afternoon so that we could go past the Root Worker's flat. It was Marcus's idea. He got tired of playing the same old games I guess. Halfway there Reverend Blackwell from the church on Charlevoix Street pulled up beside us in his new car. Spanking new Buick the Husband calls it, since the last one was a 61—black, not even two years old—and last month he bought another one. He rolled his window down and hollered out to us, "Lord sure did bless us with a fine day didn't He?"

Marcus stopped and squinted at his face in the shiny hubcaps. I tugged at his sleeve. "Can't talk to him, Marcus," I whispered.

"Was just admiring all His gifts," Reverend Blackwell went on. "Sun shining, roof over everybody's head far as I can see. Then I said, Lord look at those healthy looking kids. Clothes on their backs, shoes on their feet . . . I know you must thank Him."

We didn't say a thing.

Reverend Blackwell scratched his head. "What puzzles me though is I don't recall seeing you in church. Don't thank Him and He'll take it all away. Can't thank Him if you don't set foot in His church."

Marcus frowned and pulled me with him. "We go to Saint Agnes!" he hollered over his shoulder.

"Ain't like it's home," Reverend Blackwell called after us. "Nothing like coming back to your roots."

Seems like Reverend Blackwell's nice enough—always smiles and nods at everyone. But the Woman said he's a hypocrite, said how can somebody care about folks when he won't even live among them?

Reverend Blackwell doesn't live next door to his church like Father Ritkowski. Not even in a rectory but on the west side, Clarissa. Where the houses are brick and nobody will walk past a weed without pulling it up from the ground. The Woman said that's where people who've made something of themselves live. She said Reverend Blackwell comes this way on Sunday to preach and collect money from folks so he can pay for his house and new car. And on Fridays he comes to see what else he can get from all the people he calls himself saving.

But Aunt Della said he's a foreman at the plant, that's how he has so much. Said he marched downtown with Martin Luther King and he'll march in Washington too if his church sends him.

"Did all that and they still ain't got nothing," the Woman

said. "How they figure sending him do the same thing someplace else'll get them any different?"

Aunt Della said she's going to move to the west side too as soon as she hits a big number. I think she likes him.

The big Buick drove slowly by us and on down the street, shining silver against the dirty brown and yellow houses. Shining new against the cracked sidewalk and dried-up tree stumps the men said they'd come back for—that was when I was seven.

I watched the big car shine smooth and polished through the shadows that paint-peeling porches made in the street. It stopped beside an old white Cadillac with black and green doors and a squashed-in tail fin. Reverend Blackwell stuck his head out the window to talk to the man who squatted in front of its jacked-up front wheel.

We caught up with Marcus's friends Little Man and Eddie near the Root Worker's flat. Little Man was arguing that they shouldn't mess with her. "You'll be sorry if she put a fix on us," he said. "Cause then what can we do?"

It didn't make any sense to Eddie.

"Aw, Little Man," he said, "what would she want to do that for when all she sees is just some kids walking by?"

"But she knows," Little Man said after he thought about it a minute.

"My daddy said she don't know nothing," Eddie told him. "Except how to take a lot of dumb folks' money and stir up some shit."

I eased back and didn't say a thing, just kept my mouth shut and tried to think about sitting on the steps and talking to you, Clarissa. And I tried to think about God and going to heaven but mostly about you. Every now and then the Root Worker's face laughed inside my head. That's when I concentrated harder and I tried to see God again but all I saw was you. That was good enough.

"Then why'd Mr. Stevens drop dead like he did?" Little Man asked. "Mama said Mr. Stevens was all right before his wife got tired of his no-working ass and went to see the Root Worker. After that he couldn't hold his own pee. Next thing she knew he just up and dropped dead. Like that."

"Auntie said the Root Worker's a good woman, can fix what God *and* the doctors give up on," Marcus said.

*Oh, my God, I am heartly sorry . . .* I prayed.

"You believe that?"

"Look at old Miss Morris," Little Man went on like he knew more than any of us. "She was ate up with cancer and the doctor couldn't do a thing to fix it. They prayed but she was dying—couldn't do nothing. They took her to the Root Worker and look at her now."

*. . . and I detest all my sins, this one too . . .*

"You dumb? God did it, not her. Did a miracle."

Little Man wouldn't give up. "My mama said the Root Worker pulled live snakes right out of Miss Hettie's belly—"

"My daddy said Miss Hettie *is* a snake."

"—and she stopped the devil from taking over Mr. Gray's whole self."

"Sister said we shouldn't believe that stuff!" I screamed at them. "It's a sin!"

They all got quiet, then turned around.

"What you talking about her to Sister for anyway, Ellen?" Marcus asked. "You know Mama said don't go telling stuff."

"I didn't," I hurried up and said.

Eddie interrupted. "My uncle said it's the Root Worker who's the devil."

They kept arguing about her till we were in front of her flat.

I froze when we saw the long narrow steps that led up to her door. Twenty-two. I counted them twice this week. Twenty-two steps on the side of the empty red store with

KERCHEVAL AVENUE HARDWARE—QUALITY LAWNMOWERS written in almost invisible crayon on a sign that dangled in its window. It used to be twenty-four steps, Clarissa. Maybe twenty-five. I can tell by the big empty space between the top ones. Sometimes I imagine the steps leading to heaven like they do on television. But today my eyes followed the brick to the tiny window above the store. And then followed the last step to the heavy dark door with a yellow board nailed at the top where glass used to be.

Marcus laughed. "Counting to five," he said. "Not on Glue by five you got to go up there knock on her door—one, two . . ."

We took off, grabbing trees, leaping on grass, and screaming *Glue!* as fast as we could.

"There she is!" someone yelled and we ran like lightning. Boys hollering and girls screaming, flying off every which way, running for our lives and not looking back. I was right behind Marcus.

We made it home and fell on the front stairs. Marcus laughed and tried to catch his breath at the same time. "I didn't see anyone," he said. "You?"

I didn't see her, just ran like everyone else. Hope she didn't see me.

~

Got the Curse again.

When it first stopped I thought it left for good. But it came back again, and again this time. Goes away just to come back. The Woman said it'll happen the rest of my life and won't stop till I get too old to be any use to anyone.

I don't want to think about hiding rags, being careful no one finds them, then hauling out the oildrum and making fires. Sneaking rags out to burn twice a day every month for the rest of my life almost. How many times you think that'll be, Clarissa?

I woke up early this morning and pulled the mattress out on the upstairs porch. The Woman said someone's coming over today. She hates the smell of pee and hates it even more when she gets company. I don't like to pee the bed but I can't stop and it makes her mad.

"Ain't trying hard enough," she tells me all the time. "Just too trifling to get up and go to the bathroom."

I would get up if I could wake up and feel it, Clarissa. But the trouble is I just can't feel it. So every morning I put the sheet and blanket on the upstairs porch banister and drag the mattress out to air. I'm ashamed because they're out there where the whole world can see my trifling ways.

This morning the Woman let me wash the sheet and blanket at least. "Don't want piss hanging all over the porch where they can see it. And I don't want you dragging that smell back in this house," she said.

I washed the bed things and hung them on the line in the backyard. When I started for the steps I remembered the rag. I ran upstairs and found it on the porch where it dragged out under the mattress, still balled up in the newspaper I wrapped it in this morning. I took it out and burned it.

When I turned to go back in the house I saw an empty spot on the line where the sheet should have been but wasn't. Then I heard James under the porch. And Leslie Johnson.

"Hold still. Got to put it in." I heard him whispering loud. I went over to see.

"Shh! Somebody'll hear us, James!" Leslie sounded mad.

"Can't nobody hear us. Hold still." James spoke a little louder.

"But you never said we're going together!" She was mad.

"Can't let nobody do it if they ain't my boyfriend."

"Told you I *like* you," he said. "You know that. Else why would I be with you?"

"Get *up*, James," she said louder and madder. "You ain't serious, just want to use somebody."

I squatted and peeked in the opening straight at James's brown butt shining buck naked and up in the air hanging over Leslie's thighs. She shoved at him and then spotted me over his shoulder.

"James!" she hollered trying harder to push him up. He just laughed and kept prying at her thighs with his knee.

"Fool, somebody's looking!"

He turned his head and she scrambled to pull her drawers up over her butt that was on top of my sheet.

James frowned and hollered, "What you looking at, girl? Get out of here!"

I couldn't move.

"Get out of here, Ellen!" he hollered looking around for something. "Move, I said!"

I stared at James's naked thighs and the thing that stood straight out like a snake between them. And inside my head I watched the Root Worker pull a snake out of Miss Hettie's belly.

A rock hit my shoulder.

"You crazy *and* deaf? I said leave!" James looked around for another rock to throw.

Leslie fought to get up but James held her down with his elbow. I moved in slow motion, half crawling, half scooting away from the hole, and almost fell. I went up the steps over the crawl-hole as Leslie cried under my feet.

"Shh! Leslie," James whispered. "She's my sister, ain't nothing to be scared of. Talks to herself, I swear."

Leslie laughed. And then they were quiet.

I tried to stay away from him all day. Seems like I must have sinned. Not because I had seen what he was doing with Leslie under the stairs but because I *wanted* to see. He reminds me about it every chance he gets, moving his hips around like he's humping or something, laughing and whispering, "Leslie, Leslie," when he's close enough to do it.

This evening I watched the rest of the clothes go around in the washing machine. I didn't think about much, just let my mind go around squishing up and down with the clothes, watching the suds disappear and come back up again. I was putting the shirts through the wringer when I felt James's breath on the back of my neck.

"Leslie, Leslie," it whispered.

I almost caught my fingers in the wringer.

"Ellen, wanna see something?" he asked. He reached in his pants and pulled out his thing. I turned my head away.

"Feel it, Ellen," he whispered to my neck. He grabbed my hand and tugged. I snatched it back.

"James, are you crazy?" I whispered. "I'm telling!"

"Crazy?" He laughed. "*You* calling somebody crazy? It's you ain't wrapped too tight—who you gonna tell?"

The basement floor was cold. That's all I could feel. And then all I could see was James on top of Leslie. Leslie turned into you, Clarissa, and I watched.

~

"Ain't asked for no rag," the Woman said to me across the kitchen table.

I hadn't thought about rags for a long time, just didn't need any.

"Ain't asked for no rag," she said again. "It's been going on two months, Ellen, and you ain't asked for no rag."

*Ain't asked for a rag?*

"No, ma'am. I haven't needed any."

She bit her lip. "Who've you been laying with, Ellen?"

"Huh?"

"Who *had* you, Ellen? Who've you been laying with?" she hollered, like hollering would make me understand.

I looked around the table, first at Marcus. His eyes said he didn't understand what the Woman was talking about either. I glanced over at James and his head ducked under the table like he had lost something. *Who've you been laying with, Ellen?* I thought about the time in the basement. Not one time, but a lot of them. And once in the garage—wherever it was when he caught me by myself. I stared down at the table leg and something hard stuck in my throat.

*Who you gonna tell?* I heard him say in my head.

"Nobody," I said. "Haven't been with anyone."

"One more time, Ellen." She leaned forward. "I won't ask you but one more time."

"I don't know."

She bit her lip again. "Ought to snatch your tongue out for lying's what I ought to do. Who, Ellen!"

My throat tied itself around the hard thing that stuck in it. "James," I whispered to the floor.

"*Who?*"

Before I could repeat it, she let out a scream and came across the table like she really was going to snatch my tongue out. Chairs and plates flew everywhere. I ran for the stairs. The Woman took off behind me, calling for James and Marcus to help. And they took off behind her.

My legs almost gave out but I made it up the stairs. I could tell they were close behind because I could hear them. I finally reached the bathroom door where it would be safe—Glue. They pushed it open and I fell backward. I squatted and breathed in until I could feel myself leave the floor, and you were there instead.

The Woman's voice grated like the sound of chalk backward on a chalkboard. "Who you been with, Ellen? Who!" it screamed over and over until it faded off.

I looked down and you were all beat up and huddled on the floor near the heat vent.

I drew the outline of a bow tie on a piece of paper and colored it blue to match my skirt. Then I tore it out and fastened it to my blouse with a sewing needle. It scratched my chin so I pinned it again and felt to make sure it was on straight. After that I ran my fingers over my hair, feeling each plait for loose ends. I rebraided the fuzzy ones and caught the ends of the ones that were loose and pinned the longest one over the spot in my head where hair won't grow. When it all seemed just right I slipped out the door and ran to catch Marcus. I heard the Woman call after me, "Look at you, Ellen, that ugly look about you! You know God hates ugly. Hold your head up, might look a little better."

She has to say that every time I go outside. I don't know why—just has to.

The kids across the street echoed her.

"Hold'cha head up! . . . head up! . . . head . . ."

I ran almost a block to catch Marcus and his friends who were already playing tag. I was It again. The grass was Glue. I chased them and they ran, laughing and hollering *Glue!* every time their feet touched grass. I didn't tag anyone, never do—grass is Glue and grass is everywhere.

I stopped chasing them at the next corner when we reached Mr. Julius's store. I peeked into his window and looked for you. I knew you'd be there, staring back at me. You always wait for me there.

This time, though, you scared me. Tiny plaits stood up and

curled around your head like a thousand little Medusa snakes waiting to spring out. Eyes puffed like a big anthill, all purple-green. A red slit peeked out and divided one in half. The corner of your lip—greenish-purple too, and fat and twisted—hanging like a frown that hid the edge of your bottom lip.

I looked down at your arms, at welts that looked like giant mosquito bites, then down past your wrinkled up skirt to dirty legs with marks that matched the ones on your arms. Ugly. You were just plain ugly.

You stared back at me for a long time. Inside my head I saw you leave the window and run off to play. But then Marcus called me, so I turned from the window and ran to chase them again.

"God," we said, "is the Supreme Being Who made all things."

"And why did God make us?" Sister asked.

I raised my hand.

"Ellen?"

I stood.

"To show forth His goodness," I answered. "And to share His happiness."

She smiled. "Good, Ellen. Now excuse yourself and report to the office."

*Me?*

She read my mind.

"Mother Superior wants to talk to you."

I walked toward the front of the room and felt a hundred eyes on me. As I passed their desks they scooted over in their seats so that my clothes wouldn't brush against theirs. Sister smiled and stepped away from me too. I wanted to run. Just run away from her, the kids—from everything.

I don't understand what it means when Sister smiles at me. I know what it means for other people. For them it shows that she's happy, that something seems funny to her, even that she's just about had it. But when she smiles at me it's different. And she backs away like I have a disease. It seems like she makes up smiles for me out of her Charity vows. That she adopts a smile for me just like she has us collect money to adopt little starving African pagan babies. That's when I believe that I'm the pagan, Clarissa, and that she's saving me with a smile.

I opened the office door and stood in front of Mother Superior's desk. She looked at me for a long time and didn't say anything. I stared at the floor, then at the rust on the bottom of her file cabinet.

"Ellen," I heard her say. "Are you listening to me?"

"Yes, Sister."

She tapped her pencil against the desk. "Well, I'm waiting. Why are you such a mess this morning?"

"Me?" I asked like she might have been talking to someone else.

She sucked in her breath.

"Who else can I be talking to, Ellen? Look at you—what happened?"

"Don't know." *Always lying, Ellen.*

"Don't know?"

"Fell in some bushes," I hurried up and said.

She shook her head and folded her arms. "How'd you manage to do it this time?"

"Don't know how. Just fell, I guess."

I got mad at you, Clarissa. I wondered if God really made you, and if He did, why He made you so ugly, since He hates ugly.

~

They say it's inside me and they can tell it's growing.

I don't look like anything's in me—don't feel anything either, except a little sick every now and then. But I don't act sick when

I feel it. The Woman gets mad when I do that, says the sickness comes from what I did.

She took me to see the Root Worker last night. The Root Worker reached under my skirt and put her hand on my belly, then said she can feel that I'm about two months gone, and that it's the Husband's. The Woman told her that she knows her feeling is telling her something right because who else would I be laying with, and he hadn't laid with her in a good while. I didn't say anything about James to them.

The Woman keeps shaking her head and saying "that old dog" to herself over and over again. Sometimes she looks at me like she's ready to hit me so I try to stay out of her way. She didn't say too much else about it to me after talking to the Root Worker, except one day when she called me into the kitchen and said, "It's a disgrace, a sin and a disgrace before God, and you ought to be ashamed."

I do feel ashamed but I don't know exactly what it is I'm ashamed about.

The Root Worker told the Woman to get it out of me before I get too much further along and it's too late. She told her to wait for something that has to do with the moon, and to put down some of the powder that she gave her.

I imagine it growing inside me. I imagine its eyes first, and then its hands and legs and feet. That's all. No nose or mouth or anything else. It scares me.

Have you ever heard of a glop?

That's what I call the baby they say I imagined that I had. I call it a glop because it didn't look like a baby or anything I've ever seen, just a dark red mess not even big enough to be a baby— a glop.

Aunt Della was there when I had it, arguing with the Woman

about who its daddy might be and how messed up I must be now. Aunt Della said that what they did messed me up so I can't have any more. The Woman told her that I'm as strong as an ox and will have plenty more. I want to believe Aunt Della—it hurts too much when they take one out.

The Woman told Aunt Della that all of my babies will be ill-aformed—whatever that is—because spirits are working through me. She said the Root Worker told her one of them is her mother, and it won't leave her alone either. She said it rides me like I'm a horse, on my shoulders. And it won't quit until the horse is blind. That's me, the horse, I guess. But the Woman won't let her do anything to my eyes. She told the Root Worker she'll have to think of something—the last thing she needs is for me to be blind on top of being off and peeing in the bed.

"Guess she'll just have to keep having ill-aformed ones, then," the Woman said.

Aunt Della said they'll be that way if I keep on tapping too close to the tree too—whatever that means.

I flushed it down the toilet, just like it was shit. And then it became nothing. After I cleaned myself up they told me that it never happened—what I thought I remembered that they did, I only imagined. I believed them at first, but then I saw all of the bloody rags when I took the garbage out. And the bottom of my stomach hurts too much for it not to have happened.

Now I pretend to not know anything or remember anything.

I heard the Woman cry in the middle of last night, and then I heard her hum.

I got out of bed and followed the sound to the stairs, then looked down into the front room where she was crying and humming and cleaning all at the same time because that's what she does. When she hurts, and the hurt's bad enough to make her soul ache, she hums.

"Tears won't do a thing," she told me one day, "but humming soothes the pain." And last night she hummed while she cleaned like she could clean all of the ache away too.

I don't know much about what makes her hurt all the time. Sometimes it's just living, she says. Most times it's me. But I don't know what it is about living and about me that does that to her.

"Girl, you just don't know how hurt feels," she said to me when I told her how it hurt to walk after they took the baby out. "Knowing you carried something for all that time, and giving it birth and taking care of it all these years just to see it turn out like you. Can't tell you how it feels. Wait till you go through what I go through and then tell me how it hurts."

But I don't know what it is that made her hurt so bad this time—she won't say what it is. I watched her wince from it a few times though. And she stops what she's doing to grab her stomach and squeeze a chair or something. Tight, like she's trying to squeeze the pain away. But when the Husband's around she acts like she feels just fine.

"Better not even so much as mention to him you seen me like this," she told us.

And last night she grabbed and squeezed the end of the front room table, and she ached while she hummed and cried and cleaned it.

I followed the Woman up the long steps that led to the room over the store, carrying the big jar with my womanhood rag in it.

The short thick yellow woman answered the door in her red wig and a grin that showed one gold tooth in the middle of a row of yellowish ones. Her round face reminded me of the cherubim painted on the church walls.

She's the Root Worker.

She led us inside that dark musty room she lives in. I still can't get used to its sickening sweet smell like woman odor mixed with perfume and candle wax. It always makes me dizzy and this time I felt like throwing up.

We went behind the curtain of dusty ragged blankets that divides the room in half. There was no light in the room except for the candles that lit up the homemade altar in the center of the middle wall. Let me tell you about the altar.

It's made out of white painted woodcrates that are fading gray, and has jars of perfumed candles and oil on it. Tiny brown packets of powder are lined up in neat rows in front of the oil, along with what looks like half-burned hair and black bird feathers.

Do you remember when I told you that the lady who ran the beautyshop down the street died? The Root Worker has a picture of that lady hanging above the altar right next to a tiny picture of the Woman's mother. She calls them souls. She said she lights a candle there every night to keep them trapped inside their likeness.

A card table and chairs are in the middle of the room and a small cooking stove is near the other wall. She uses the oven to heat the room and to dry things for root working. I don't know if she uses the stove for cooking too—I never saw her cook on it.

A toilet's near another wall. Just that. There's no sink or tub. Just a toilet all by itself with no curtain around it or door to close. Right where everyone in the room can see what anyone is doing on it.

The dead beautyshop lady's husband was there. He lay on a naked mattress on the side of the room where the stove is. He's a little skinny man, dark with feet that look too big for his body. He had nothing on but his drawers. They say that he married the Root Worker about five or six months ago, but it still seemed funny seeing him there with nothing on but his drawers.

He got up and pulled his pants on a few minutes after we got there. He laughed and talked with the Woman for a while—I couldn't hear what they said to each other—then he went to the other side of the blanket curtain.

The Root Worker played with my plaits while she talked to the Woman.

"Shame, working on you through this here child," she said. "A low down shame. Don't be thinking I ain't seen nothing like this though, cause I have. Plenty of times, mostly back when I was down south with Robert Earl 'nem's folks."

She stopped playing with my plaits and leaned over and stared into my face like she was trying to find something on it. I tried to make the shape of something out of the little brown spots on the bottom oven door. Then she put her face close to mine and twisted her head sideways so that her eye almost touched mine. She must have found what she was looking for—she finally stood up.

"Trying to get back at you's what she's doing," she told the Woman, sounding like she was satisfied that she'd found it. "Get back at you and take your husband from you too's what she wants now. Ain't gonna stop neither, not till he's hers."

The Woman frowned at me like I was the "she" that the Root Worker was talking about. She turned back to the Root Worker with a worried look. The Root Worker smiled.

"That's all right though," she said to the Woman. "Got something for you that can fix anything."

She stared at the Woman and thought for a minute.

"Twenty-five," she said. "You a good woman—only twenty-five this time."

The Woman pulled some money from her brassiere and counted it, shaking her head slowly while the Root Worker watched.

The Root Worker rubbed her elbows and thought again. "Okay," she said. "Owe me the other five. You good for it."

The Woman let out her breath and gave the money to her.

The Root Worker told me to give her the jar that I had for-gotten I was still holding. I handed it to her, ashamed that my rag was in it.

She ran her fingers along the outside of the jar.

"Evil," she said while her fingers felt the jar. "Feels evil all over this here thing. Nothing but evil." She turned the jar over, touched it, and moaned while she stared at the rag inside. She closed her eyes. "Yes!" she all of a sudden said out loud. "She's working on you, all right. Fixing you but real good." She opened her eyes and gave the Woman a sorrowful look. "Baby, they fixing you," she half whispered. "Wonder you ain't gone already. Got a fix on you so, can't nobody do nothing about it but me."

The Woman looked like she was ready to cry. The Root Worker took her hand.

"Might've killed you," she said. "Already been with your hus-band—can tell that just by looking at it. You'd been stone cold dead, baby, and they'd been on about their business, hear me?"

The Woman nodded and bit her lip.

"Sit on down here," the Root Worker led her to the table.

She motioned for me to sit down, then disappeared behind the blanket and came back holding a jar with something in it that looked like tea, and two cups. She poured some of the stuff into the cups, closed her eyes, and touched both cups and moaned. Then she made a shape on one of them with her finger and sat it down in front of me.

"Here," she said, pushing the cup to me. "Drink it all down."

I thought about hell.

"Won't hurt you," she said. "Just drink it so I can help her."

I thought about the Woman—how she had gone from one doctor to another and told them how sick she was, how her stom-ach ached so bad she could barely make it at times. They never found what was wrong with her, said it was in her head.

I picked the cup up and looked inside it. I thought about how it's a sin to believe in the Root Worker. So I told myself I didn't believe. But I was scared. And I was sorry that I was there doing something pagan just because I was scared. Sister said that sometimes our faith is tested. That's when we find out if we really believe in God. I guess that's why you weren't there, Clarissa—my faith was being tested.

I didn't drink it. I put the cup down and tried to whisper to the Woman what Sister had said about what we were doing. She jumped up from her chair and slapped me.

"Sister, shit!" she screamed. "Don't go telling me nothing about what a damn Sister said." She stood close with her fists balled like she was going to hit me again. "What the hell you think the Sisters can do for me? Can't do nothing, fool!"

The Root Worker shook her head as she came around to my side of the table. She pulled the Woman from me, then rubbed my shoulders. "Child's stubborn," she said. "Baby, you need to break this child—too much spirit in her." She picked the cup up and motioned to the Woman. "Here," she said. "Just hold her down."

The Woman held me down in the chair while the Root Worker poured the stuff into my mouth. It was nasty, bitter, like medicine and salt mixed with something else that I've never tasted. It went down my throat, choking me. Some spilled down the side of my neck and down my collar.

"There." The Root Worker rubbed my back. "See? What'd I tell you? Fighting and carrying on for nothing. Ain't never hurt nobody."

She poured the rest of the stuff in another cup, and told the Woman to drink it. The Woman cut her eyes at me then turned the cup up quickly. It was nasty to her too, I could tell.

The Root Worker went over to the altar and came back with a lit white candle and one of the tiny packets. She moved the candle around the jar, singing something that I couldn't understand. She blew it out and unscrewed the lid. Then she placed the jar beneath her dress, squatted over it, and peed.

The Root Worker poured the rest of the brown stuff into the jar and sprinkled powder from the packet around the outside and shook it.

She sat the jar in front of me and nodded.

I thought about the pee in the jar and about mortal sin and hell.

I pushed the chair away from the table and ran toward the curtain, holding my hand tight against my mouth. She grabbed me before I could make it to the other side and pulled me back to the table.

The Woman shook her head and stared at me as though she had seen something on me that she didn't believe was there. The thought of whatever it was moved across her eyes and twisted her face, then moved down to her hands. She balled them into fists as tight as her twisted face. A sound came up in her throat and stuck, and she pushed it through her tightened lips, and it grew into a scream.

"You *want* to kill me!" it said. "You *want* me to die!" And she let her fists loose with the sound—in my face, in my chest—everywhere.

My head pounded and I tasted blood. Then I felt my tooth— the one that's not here anymore—with my tongue, pushing it in and back out again until it finally fell out and rolled under the table.

I thought about you and the martyrs. I didn't want to hurt like you or suffer like the martyrs, so I picked up the jar and drank from it and prayed in my head.

I gagged and it came out all over the table.

The Woman heaved and ran for the toilet, choking and throwing up too. Mess was all over the place. The Root Worker stood over her while she knelt over the toilet. She patted her on the back and hummed calmly the whole time.

"It's coming," she said. "Lord knows, it's coming out." She looked back at me and smiled, then turned back to the Woman. "All them snakes and evil they put on you, it's all coming out," she said. "Can't hurt you now."

I sat up in bed all night, scared that I would die and burn in hell for all of eternity. Scared of the quiet that was so loud it seemed to gnaw away at me. And I was surrounded by something—spirits, I guess—that tried to make me become a part of something that wasn't myself. I became too heavy to move, but my insides tossed around like they were trying to find the rest of the something that I had become a part of.

You weren't there, Clarissa. I searched for you and you weren't there. Gone. Maybe because my soul was mine, not yours, and I had lost faith.

I knelt inside the Confessional and the Root Worker's face came into my head. Big. Then, what had happened yesterday—all of it—inside my head. I hurried up and changed my thought in case it might have been another sin.

The little window opened.

"Bless me, Father, for I have sinned," I said to the shadow on the other side of the window.

~

A cila lady moved into Mr. Stevens's flat across the alley.

I don't know much about her except that's what the old lady next door said she must be—a *cila*. I couldn't find it in the dictionary but I like the way it sounds, like music or dancing or something. And I imagine the Cila Lady in a long silver dress singing long slow songs, and people who dance like blue swans in a dream. Silver-blue like the tiny car that the Cila Lady folds up into as if she's packing herself away.

"Must not have anybody," the Woman said when she watched the Cila Lady fold out of her car. "No husband, no kids. Never did see any. Must not plan on having any. Wouldn't make much sense to have that little piece of nothing."

"Got to have some man somewhere," Aunt Della told her. "Else how could she come up with a car? But even all by herself it still don't make much sense—all that ass and legs a mile long. Looks like she'd get one that fits."

I think it fits just right. I like to watch her unfold out of it like it's a secret sort of box and she's the only one who knows exactly how to make herself the perfect size to get in and out of it.

She doesn't look like a husband-and-kids lady, Clarissa. She wears straight skirts and high heels with her toes out. And she wears toenail polish and long earrings all the time, with eye-glasses, like she must be fast and smart at the same time. Like her name should be Miss Irene—that sounds fast and smart. Her hair is always fixed too. Sometimes real short with tight shiny curls—Aunt Della said they're called crokono style or something—sometimes tight on top and long and wavy in back. Aunt Della said it's a piece. I like it when it's long and wavy in back.

Nobody ever says anything to the Cila Lady. Aunt Della said they have to keep their mouths shut and their men away from her and just watch and listen out for something. The Woman and the old lady next door sometimes watch her from the alley fence together. Sometimes she waves when she sees them, and they'll wave back a little, but the Woman says, "Well, I have to go see about those kids," out loud when it looks like the Cila Lady might want to come over to talk to them.

She waved at me when I took the boxes out for the junk man, and I wanted to ask her if her name was Irene, but I thought someone might tell, so I pretended that I didn't see her until the junk man stopped to talk to her.

"Umph! Lord help that man if he has a wife," I heard the old lady next door say out loud to nobody. "Lord help him if he do!"

The Woman said that the doctors plucked Mrs. Stevens's insides from her just like you'd pluck gizzards from a chicken. Had to do it. Something was done to her to make her inside woman parts drive her crazy. And it all has something to do with the Cila Lady, she said.

"First Thomas Stevens dropping dead like he did," she said to Aunt Della. "Then what happened to his wife wasn't even a year after that. And her moving away all of a sudden. And ain't it funny that *she* moves into the very flat where all that went on—by herself in all that house, and nobody ever saw a rent sign."

"Never was right after that—Jessie Stevens," Aunt Della said. "Walked around with her eyes looking just as empty as inside of herself was. Wonder what became of her? Heard she wasn't any more good for a man. That's why her new husband ran off. House paid for, kids grown, had a new Buick with the insurance she got from Thomas's death—it's a shame when a man ain't worth shit till he's dead—and Jessie still couldn't hold on to a husband. Heard he said it was just like falling into a big empty hole. Couldn't feel nothing. And that woman over there now—ain't never saw a for rent sign, nothing. Just a big truck pull up from nowhere, full of stuff and her."

Aunt Della was quiet for a minute, then said, "Ain't it funny how it was *both* of'm? Never heard of both, ain't no reason. What I want to know is how come?"

The Woman bit her lip. "Della, you can't hear for listening to yourself talk," she said. "That's how they say cilas *do*. They put their selves on a man and make him come down with something so heavy he drops dead. Then as soon as his wife gets to feeling a little bad they take what the husband did to her sick bed. It makes his wife come down sicker than she was till she's to the point of death. And she'll die too if she don't get help quick. Even if she gets help, what he did is still on her in the same place that the cila used to make the husband heavy. And it stays there heavy on the wife this time. It presses down till it makes her so crazy out of her head it kills her. That's why they had to pluck Jessie's woman parts out. It was all that they could do."

"You still ain't said how she'd come to get Jessie too."

The Woman turned around quick and got so close to Aunt Della's face I thought she would hit her. I think Aunt Della had the same thought because she flinched.

"Cause she's a *cila*, I told you, Della. That's what cilas *do*. Now, asking me how come a cila would do what's in her nature to do is the same as asking me how come evil does what's evil. Ask the ones that told us about that woman."

I watch the Cila Lady every chance I get. And when I don't get a chance, I make one up—find stuff to take to the alley, sweep the backporch and yard so I can sweep my way to the alley fence. And I take the garbage out all day long—"Ellen sure is getting funny about garbage in the house," the Woman says—just to get a chance to see her. And she doesn't seem to mind that I never wave back. She waves every time she looks up and sees me, just like she waves to everyone else who acts like they don't want to talk to her.

Yesterday she came straight across the alley and held a little blue and green striped bag over the fence. "Hey, young lady," she called. I knew she was calling to me. No one else was around.

I liked the way she called me a young lady, but I kept sweeping.

"Here's a little something I picked up for you," she called.

I leaned the broom against the tree and went over to the fence. She stretched the bag out to me.

"Kind of looked like you. Thought you might like it."

I pinched the sides of the bag together and rolled the top down tight to keep from looking inside.

"Thank you," I said and waited for her to go back down the alley. But she just looked at me like she was trying to figure something out.

"Ever take those plaits down?" she asked.

I let my eyes follow a big green stripe around the bag.

"No, ma'am," I answered. "Just when I plait them again."

"Well, I'd like to fix those in your hair," she nodded at the bag. "Take those plaits down, curl it. What do you think?"

I thought about some of those shiny crokono curls in my hair and that she must have put a long wavy piece like hers in the bag. I thought I'd look good and everyone would say, "Can that be Ellen?" I thought I should turn around and run.

"Can't. I have to go somewhere," I said. I started to turn like I was in a hurry, but the Cila Lady just leaned closer against the fence.

"Well, I didn't say it has to be today," she said.

*Combs. One shiny blue and one yellowish white with see-through teeth that look like skinny little windows. Diamonds should be in the white one, so I imagine that they're there. Tiny ones all around the edge of the comb, shining as silver as I think the Cila Lady's singing dress must be.*

I stuck the blue one on the end of a middle plait and imagined that it held the hairpiece I had hoped the Cila Lady had given me. I plaited thread from my blouse sleeve through the teeth of the white one, and squinted to see what it looked like.

"If you don't get out from under there!"

I snatched the comb out and scrambled to raise my head from under the blanket.

"Don't think I don't know what you're up to under there!"

The Woman snatched the rest of the blanket back, and I threw the combs under the bed at the same time.

"Ain't two seconds off you and look what you do!"

I scrambled to my feet. She smelled the blanket, then threw it down.

"Just send you to make beds and you all up in yourself. Now go wash this thing!"

I started to pick it up.

"Go wash your hands," she said. "Don't touch nothing else till you do!"

Aunt Della said that Jessie Stevens had a knot that was as big as a garlic clove. She said it was a pea at first, then she noticed it grew a little bigger every time her new husband got with her. That's how they knew it must have come from what had been put on her dead husband. Jessie Stevens never was a heavy bleeder, Aunt Della said. But she bled so much one month her womanhood rag couldn't hold it. Towels couldn't hold it either, and it put her in the sick bed. But it didn't feel like sick, she said—just weak and tired. Seven or eight days later it almost stopped, but her new husband couldn't wait so she let him have her right on the sick bed. It started again, just like a faucet.

"Dogs don't care," the Woman said. "That should have told Jessie something wasn't right with him either."

Three weeks later the little knot came, and it was almost a year to the day that Mr. Stevens died. She wouldn't go to the Root Worker but her old mother went for her.

"Tell Jessie it's on her now," the Root Worker said. "She knows where to come."

Her mother told her but she still didn't go. Aunt Della told the Woman that she didn't know why but it must have been something about Mr. Stevens's death that kept his wife from asking the Root Worker for help. I sort of think she didn't want to drink the pee stuff, but I acted like I didn't know why either.

Jessie Stevens tried to help herself though. Aunt Della said she wouldn't let her new husband near her after that. But the knot grew anyway and she bled until it drove her crazy and almost killed her. That's when her new husband took her to have her woman parts plucked out.

I tiptoed upstairs and took the yellow-white comb out from under the bed. Dust made the thread into a caterpillar that I didn't want to touch. I blew it and wiped it with a sock until it was thread again. I unplaited the thread from around the teeth and thought about the Cila Lady. And Mrs. Stevens's knot. Then I squeezed my eyes until I looked straight through her empty insides and saw James standing where their end should have been. I tied a hundred little knots in the thread, then knotted it all around the Cila Lady's comb.

"Still won't let me do that hair?" the Cila Lady asked.

I pulled a handful of long skinny weeds from under the fence.

"No, ma'am—got to go someplace pretty soon."

"If you liked the combs you didn't tell me."

"Yes, ma'am . . . I mean, I like them."

"Could have fooled me. Almost a month and ain't seen them in your head yet."

I tied one of the weeds in a knot around a fence link.

"Yes, ma'am, I save them for dress up."

She scrunched her nose like something was on her mind. "Never saw you dressed up. You ought to let me take you to church. It'll be good for you. Then I can see how you'd look."

"I already go to church," I said. "Saint Agnes."

"Agnes? Ain't it that big Catholic church over near the plant?"

"No, ma'am, it's next to my school."

"Never knew any of us that was Catholic," she said to herself. "I belong to True Tabernacle myself. Little storefront down on Chene. Ever been there?"

"No, ma'am."

"Don't go much, maybe every other month. Guess I should and take you with me. The Catholic ones are dead. Tabernacle's not much to look at but it's got life. Always taking up collections, the only thing—that's why I don't go much." She laughed. "Had a building fund for thirteen years and ain't even close to building anything. But they all take your money, except the Catholic ones. Do they ever ask you for money?"

"No, ma'am, but they take up collections."

"Bet they don't look at you funny like they do at Tabernacle when you don't put something in. Catholic ones don't need it. Heard they get all kinds of money from some rich man over in Italy. Seems like it might make sense to go to one when you need a church but get tired of giving. Is that why you go?"

"No, ma'am. I don't want to go to hell."

"Well you can keep out of hell and have a good time doing it at Tabernacle," she said. "See if I can take you."

"Can't."

"Look, I'll take some of your folks too. Borrow my boy-friend's car to do it if it'll make you feel all right. Think they might come?"

I pulled another weed from my fist.

"No, ma'am."

She reached over and pulled the weed from my hand then tied it around the same fence link that I was going to tie it around.

"Tell me no and ain't even asked," she laughed. "How do you know?"

"Cause they said you're a cila."

"Cila?" She frowned and scrunched her nose. I wanted to snatch what I had said back.

"I won't ask you then," she said. "Must be one of those Catholic things."

The Woman had a fight with the lady next door. Not with the old lady but with the fat one who lives on the other side of us. It started when she accused the fat lady of throwing root powder into our yard, then called her a fat-assed, snuff-dipping, nappy-headed bitch. The lady came off her porch and spit snuff right in the Woman's face and the fight began. The Husband went out and tried to break it up but the Woman and the fat lady jumped on him and fought each other too. The Husband just gave up and broke away and came into the house to watch the fight with me. A whole crowd of people had gathered around by then, including Aunt Della.

When the Woman realized that the fat lady was getting the best of her, she screamed for Aunt Della to get a knife. But someone jumped on Aunt Della before she could even leave. Pretty soon the whole crowd was fighting and cussing at each other about all kinds of things that they had always wanted to tell each other about, I guess, but hadn't.

The police came and broke the whole mess up. When they asked what started it, nobody said anything. So they made everyone go home and that was the end of it.

There's so much going on around here, so many fights, so much suspicion. It seems that almost everyone is working roots, including the Woman, accusing and fixing each other for whatever. And then turning around and getting themselves unfixed from what they believe has been worked on them.

The Woman told Aunt Della that she sometimes pretends to be asleep at night so that the Husband will go to sleep before she does. While he's sleeping she hangs her drawers over his head. It helps weaken the roots of anyone who tries to fix her through him. And hanging her drawers over his head, she said, even keeps him from leaving her when he fools around with other women.

The Husband puts root powder down too when he thinks the Woman's not around or paying attention. Then *she* sprinkles root powder in rooms where the Husband has been to ward off the powder that he puts down. And they are both careful to hide their drawers from each other. They believe that some of the most powerful roots can be worked through the person who wears them.

The old people next door even work roots. That's pretty hard to believe since they're always at Mass on Sunday and everyone in the parish likes them. But they do. And there's always a root war going on between their house and ours. It seems to be the only time that the Woman and the Husband are on each other's sides.

The root wars only happen late at night when everyone else is sleeping. On most of those nights I lay awake listening to them. The old people next door dig near the fence that separates their house from ours. I can hear the water run through the hose when they fill the hole they've dug with roots, and then I hear the scraping of the shovel again when they move the dirt back into the hole. Later I can hear the Woman and the Husband whisper while they dig up the roots that the old people have planted and then plant their own. And on the nights when I stay up late, I pretend to be busy while I strain my ears to hear what they are whispering when they spy on the old couple through the dining room window.

In the daytime they all act as though what had happened the night before didn't happen. They laugh and talk to each other across the same fence that they had planted roots beside. And they even drive to Mass together after they've planted roots.

I wonder why they're not afraid of hell. I even wonder some-times if hell is just another place for root working.

Going to church with the Cila Lady was on my mind all day. First at Mass when they passed the collection basket by me. Then it was on my mind when Sister passed out the boxes of little col-lection envelopes that remind me of the Root Worker's powder packets. The collection envelopes are the ones I put notes to you in sometimes, Clarissa.

"Some of us aren't turning them in," Sister said out loud when she passed a box to me.

Sister said we're going to a cathedral for Confirmation. Blessed Sacrament Cathedral. A cathedral is much larger than Saint Agnes, she said. It's where the Archbishop says Mass. It's in the middle of places next to God. First there's the church, then the cathedral, then the Holy Father's Seat in Rome, that's closest.

"What about a tabernacle?" I asked.

She looked up over her glasses at me. "Tabernacle?"

"Yes, Sister."

"What made you bring up a tabernacle?"

"I want to go to True Tabernacle," I said. "Over on Chene Street."

"Ellen, it's not *Catholic*. A church that's not Catholic is not true and holy, and you shouldn't go to one."

I looked out the window and saw the cathedral inside the tree across the street—huge and red-orange. And the Archbishop looking like God and the Holy Father because he probably is. I saw the Cila Lady laughing with me, and all her friends having a good time inside True Tabernacle. I wondered if God would strike all of us down inside the little storefront.

The Woman is so pretty.

She let me watch her comb her hair yesterday. I think I'm

something when she calls me into the room to keep her company while she does her hair. Just the two of us, like we're best friends and she needs me to talk to because I'm the only one in the world who can really understand her. She said that sometimes talking to me makes her feel like it's her mother that she's talking to because I have her mother's eyes. She loved her mother's eyes and hated her for taking them away.

Those eyes, she told me, used to look at her just like they knew everything about her—how she felt, what she thought, every time she hurt and where—without a word being said. And they used to look at her for no reason sometimes in an admiring sort of way, telling her that they knew she was pretty, that they knew she would be beautiful.

So when the Woman combs her hair to look especially pretty, she calls me into the room to watch. And I make my eyes tell her that she's pretty again, while she tells me about just how she really feels and how she aches and where. The whole time I think about how she said men used to fight over her. I think about her long thick hair and long pretty legs, and pretend that she's a movie star and that I'm the Husband falling in love with her.

The Woman's not in love with the Husband though, said she'd leave him in a minute if she didn't have us. She really can't stand him now, since his good factory job ran out and he had to take a job emptying garbage cans at the hospital.

"You ain't no man," she told him last week. "All you good for's begging and pleading and sniffing up under me. Then cause I don't give you no ass you go to crying the blues all the time. Ain't seen your dick since God knows when," she told him. "Might not even have one for all I know."

But I like the Husband. I made a birthday card for him that said he's the most handsome man in the world. I gave it to him when the Woman wasn't here, so she wouldn't get mad. He cried when he read it. I thought he cried because it made him sad but he said it made him happy.

The Woman pulled her hair back, twisted it, and turned her face toward me. "Think this way looks better?" she smiled.

"Yes, ma'am," I answered. But every way she combed it looked pretty to me.

"You know," she said, looking in the dresser mirror, "my hair used to be so long—all the way down my back so I could almost sit on it. Having kids broke it off. Almost took my figure too. Ain't as pretty as I used to be. Used to knock'm all dead. Used to dress too—hand me that brush over there. Honey, but didn't I dress? Looked better than most of'm put together. He came along, kids came along, and it all went like that."

I imagined that I was the Woman—that I tossed my long hair and danced. That I was beautiful and a whole lot of men waited in a long line just to dance with me.

"Cleaned the stove real good last night," she said, changing the subject. "And the dining room too. Must've been up all night again. Told you taking you with me to do day work that time would give you experience. Now you got it. Can clean anywhere—kitchen shows that."

"Yes, ma'am," I said, trying to get my thought back, wishing she hadn't taken it away.

She laid the brush down and turned toward me with a sorrowful look. "You been so good these past days," she said. "But you still pisses in the bed. Lord knows when you gonna stop, girl." She shook her head and went on like she had forgotten that I was there and was really talking to the mirror. "Don't know what I'm gonna do with you," she said. "Ain't no decent man gonna have you cause you been ruined. You just dissipated your life and ruined yourself."

She looked away from the mirror and back at me. "That's why you need to know how to clean. So you'll find work and take care

of all your kids." She shook her head again like she could see all
the kids I'm going to have. "You gonna have a house full of'm,
cause you're already breeding. Gonna have'm just as sure as I'm
sitting here today. Now who's gonna want you?"

I shrugged my shoulders. I don't know who's going to want
me, Clarissa.

"Keep on working like you do," she went on. "Maybe somebody'll give you a good word so you can find some work . . ."

Long Suffering.

I need to talk to you about Long Suffering, Clarissa. It's
been on my mind since we learned about it in Catechism last
week. It's supposed to be a beatitude or grace or something, I
think. There's eight of them: "Charity, Joy, Peace, Patience,
Benignity, Goodness, *Long Suffering*, Mildness . . ." It's something like being good and holy and like God. Whatever it is, it's
the seventh one.

What I don't understand is how can a lot of suffering be good
when God was supposed to have made us to share His happiness?
Are we supposed to be happy about suffering in the same way that
everyone seems to be so happy about working roots?

I really don't understand about a lot of the holy stuff, mostly
about the martyrs and how they drove stakes through their own
hands and let themselves be flogged just to prove that they loved
God. And all of the pictures of them suffering show them twisted
up with sweat and pitiful looks. I keep thinking it must be a stupid thing to do—let yourself suffer for a long time just to prove
something. But I won't tell Sister.

How does it feel to *suffer?* I think it's a lot worse than just
hurting—that's what the Woman calls worse. "Lord, can't take
all this suffering no more," she says. It seems that what happens
to you sometimes should be called suffering too, Clarissa.
Seems like you'd say the same thing—can't take this suffering—

like the Woman. But you don't say anything, just suffer long
like the martyrs.

~

Well, Clarissa, I think I might have seen everything, but I
might not have seen anything.

The Woman sent me to ask Aunt Della to plait my hair. I
don't like Aunt Della. She always tells the Woman what she would
whip me for if I were hers. But I was glad that she wanted her to
plait my hair because she said that Aunt Della's blessed with growing hands. Maybe now my hair might grow.

I told Aunt Della what the Woman wanted, and she just
laughed and said that they had a falling out yesterday and that the
Woman really sent me because it's bad luck for a woman to be the
first one to step inside your house on New Year's Day.

"And who can be worse luck than you?" she asked me.

Still, she took me to her kitchen, told me to sit on the floor
between her knees, and began to take my plaits down. Then out
of the clear blue she told me that she had two things—a woman's
and a man's—and asked if I wanted to see them. I wanted to but
didn't say so. The Woman said that if a woman looks at another
woman's private parts it'll bring bad luck upon her whole house.
But Aunt Della lifted her skirt anyway and opened her knees wide
and told me to turn around. I turned and looked straight at it. I
knew it wasn't a man's because I had seen one of them before. She
must have known that—she was there when I had the baby. I had
also seen the Woman's when she used to sit me between her legs
to plait my hair when I was little. But Aunt Della's was longer than
the Woman's and mine put together.

After she showed it to me she didn't have anything else to say.
She just finished combing and plaiting my hair, then lit the stove
and took the hair that had broken off in the comb and burned it

on the fire. She cut some hair from her private part and put it with my burned hair into a little paper bag. Then she reached into her brassiere and pulled out a brown powder packet like the ones that the Woman buys from the Root Worker. She poured the powder into the bag of hair and gave it to me to take to the Woman.

The Woman took one look into the bag and ran into the kitchen, crying and cursing and asking God why He didn't just take her away from all of this hell.

I cried because she was crying.

# THE WATER

I DIDN'T SEE YOU YESTERDAY.

Just as I was about to look in the window for you, Mr. Julius came out of his store and told me to come inside. He scared me at first, but then he laughed and I knew it was all right.

"Know you cold, gal," he said. "Come on in here and get yourself warm."

"Might be late for school if I do, Mr. Julius," I said.

"Don't take but a minute to warm up," he said. "Need to talk to somebody about my granddaughter, you put me so much in the mind of her."

The grownups have always said that I look just like I could be some kin to Mr. Julius's wife, only she's a whole lot older and a heck of a lot better looking. I saw her a few times when we stopped in the store and she is sort of good-looking. She's about forty-something and wears fancy red dresses and perfume all the time and calls everyone Shugah Thang except for Mr. Julius. She calls him her Big Sweet-Dicked Niggah. Mr. Julius told her she shouldn't call him that around the kids who come in the store. But I can tell he likes her to call him that because he grins every time she does. Aunt Della said that Mrs. Julius is scandalous and wants all the men around here to know what she will do with a man. "Just advertising," she calls it.

People say that Mr. Julius's daughter's not his because she doesn't look like either of them but looks just like the man Mrs. Julius used to go with before she married Mr. Julius. They say that the girl he calls his granddaughter is not his real grand-daughter but is Mrs. Julius's child by a man she ran off with when he was in the service. And when the girl turned thirteen or so, Mrs. Julius sent her to live down in Alabama with her sister. The Woman said there's something funny about that too because that's the exact age the older girl—who was sup-posed to have had the granddaughter—was when Mrs. Julius sent her down there.

"And they're supposed to be so crazy about kids," the Woman said.

But they're always nice to Marcus and me, so we don't care about what people have to say about them.

I followed Mr. Julius inside and he gave me his coffee. He asked me how the Woman and the Husband were and said that they were fine people but it's a shame for them to treat me the way they do. When he said that, I almost dropped the coffee cup. I didn't know he even *knew* them, much less anything about how they treated me.

"They don't really treat me the way people say they do," I told him. But I really don't know what people say about the way they treat me.

He said, "Well if my granddaughter was here this day—and you can ask anybody—I'd treat her just as nice as I could and she wouldn't have to want for a thing. Just love the ground she walks on, she's so cute. Just like you." And he winked at me.

I never thought anyone would think I look anywhere near decent, much less cute. But he winked at me again when I got up to leave, and told me that I can stop in and have coffee with him anytime I want to.

Guess what? I *feel* pretty cute.


I went inside the store and drank coffee with Mr. Julius again. We had to sit in the little room behind the counter this time. Mr. Julius said the store doesn't open until nine and people might see us and think it's open.

He gave me a little flower pin that he had bought for Mrs. Julius just before she had left him again. I didn't know she had left him until he told me this morning. He said that if his granddaughter were here he'd have given it to her, but I'm the next best so he wanted me to have it. I told him I'd get in trouble if I took something home, so he put the pin in the drawer behind the counter and told me I could come in and put it on anytime I felt like it. I daydreamed all day at school about putting the pin on and Mr. Julius telling me how pretty I looked wearing it. I imagined that I wore a red dress just like what Mrs. Julius might wear and that Mr. Julius asked me to be his girlfriend and kissed me like they do on television. And there was music and everything.


"Nice legs," Mr. Julius said. "Umm um, gal! You got some nice fine stockings on you!" He leaned over and felt one of my legs. I pulled it away.

"Yes, *Lord!*" he said straightening back up again but still look-ing at my legs. I wanted to make them disappear.

"These is the nicest, finest legs I ever seen on a gal yet," he went on, looking down like he was talking to them. "Good stock here, corn fed stock. Granddaughter's got some nice ones too but not nice as yours. Must have plenty of boys talking to you, don't you?"

I thought about the Little Monkeyshine Boy, but the only time he talks to me is when he wants to copy my homework at recess. That's not the kind of talking Mr. Julius meant either.

"No," I said to him. "No boys ever talk to me."

"Can't believe that!" he said like I had just told a big lie. "You mean to tell me *none* of'm?"

I shook my head.

"Can't believe it." He shook his head. "Must be fools, a fine gal like you. Got a pretty nice shape too." He winked at me when he said it and I almost went through the floor. That made him laugh. "Didn't think I could tell you got a shape up under all those big clothes you be wearing, did you?"

I shook my head. I don't know what kind of shape I have, didn't want him to know.

"And what's that I see sprouting out under that shirt?" He reached out to touch one of my titties. I hurried up and covered it with my arm.

"Wasn't gonna get fast with you," he said like I had hurt his feelings. "Can't tell when I'm playing?"

"Can't do that though, Mr. Julius," I said still covering my tittie with my arm.

He tucked his head. "Don't tell me you ain't been letting nobody pull on'm," he said. "Ain't like I even want to do that— just feel'm, that's all. The way they hanging, *somebody's* got to be pulling on'm, and sucking on'm too. Been a friend to you and can't even let me feel—just do that much."

I didn't want Mr. Julius or anyone to feel them or suck them. I pulled my chest in to make them disappear.

"Gal," he said, "don't get to acting all shy and shit with me like you ain't never did nothing. I know about you and that baby you was carrying."

I froze.

"Won't get no further than you and me in this store, I swear."

He stepped back and eased down in his chair. "I won't get fast with you."

I stared at the floor.

"Look," he said, "I won't do nothing you ain't ready to do—like you too much for that. I wasn't really gonna touch you, just feel through your shirt, that's all." He grinned. "Now what can be so wrong about touching a shirt?"

It just felt wrong.

"But I won't do it, now, if you don't want me to," he said quickly. "You still my gal friend?"

I put my arms down and nodded.

"But you just be looking so *good*, gal," he said. "Now look at what you did to me."

He pointed at his thing that was sticking up inside his pants and I turned my head. He just laughed. "You sure do have some queer ways about you, gal," he said still laughing. "But that's what I like about you too. Reminds me of my granddaughter sure enough." He stopped laughing and frowned. "But it hurts so *bad*, gal, being like this," he said. "You gotta help me—might take up a bad cramp, might break off. You don't wanna see Mr. Julius hurt like this."

I stared down at it. I didn't want to, but I wondered how it would break.

"Won't even touch you, like I promised," he stood up and held my shoulders. "Just let me show you."

His voice was thick on my neck as he leaned me against the wall and grabbed my titties through my blouse, squeezing them through his fingers the way the Woman kneads biscuit dough. He rolled his belly and thighs against me and humped like he was doing it, saying, "Oowooh, shit! It feels so good," and "You know you like it, baby, ain't it good?"

I didn't answer, just wished that he would hurry up and finish humping on me because my titties hurt and the back of my head ached from pounding against the wall.

He humped faster and my head hit the wall harder. All the time he kept saying, "You wet, baby? Did I get you wet?"

I didn't know. My drawers were still wet from peeing in the bed the night before.

Mr. Julius got through and wiped the front of his pants off. He sat back down and wiped the sweat off his neck with his hand and said, "*Wooh!* I needed that!"

Then he looked over at me and frowned. "Now, you can't say I had you, gal, cause that was just a dry fuck," he said. "So anything you come up with, it wasn't from me, understand?"

I looked away and didn't answer.

"Now get out of here!" he hollered, and I ran out as fast as I could.

I didn't go in the store with Marcus after school. Mr. Julius stood in the doorway like he always does when we go past. But he didn't ask me to come in this time like he always does, just pretended he didn't see me. He talked and teased with Marcus and everyone else. I sort of stood back and felt like a sin and a toilet.

I stood in the middle of the dining room and twisted the fuzz on the spot in my head where hair won't grow. Inside my head I traced the map of some place I just made up that was carved out of the torn spot in the linoleum. James and Marcus fixed their eyes on me like they thought that same map might have been on me.

"Just wanted a man again, didn't you?" the Woman screamed at me. "Just had to have yourself a man again! Didn't care whose it was, just *had* to have one!"

"No, ma'am," I said. I hoped she'd change her mind and tell me she had made a mistake.

But she pulled the hem of my skirt up and showed me. Some

of the stuff that had come out of Mr. Julius was still on it, dried
and white.

"Proves what you did," she said. "And ain't got sense enough
not to let everybody see."

I didn't want anyone to see, just wanted to snatch my skirt
back down. But I just stood and let them see.

"Ain't got no shame about yourself," the Woman went on so
everyone could hear what she thought about me. "Too trifling to
wash it off. Walking around here looking like who knows *what*
had you. Guess that makes you happy, huh? Won't be long and
you'll mess around and breed yourself another one of my husband's babies."

"But he *didn't*," I said.

The Woman pulled my skirt all the way up and the dried stuff
touched my nose. "Then how'd you think it got here?" She shook
it in my face. "Think I'm so stupid I was born yesterday?"

"Baby, she told you the truth," I heard the Husband say from
nowhere it seemed. He stretched his arms out like he wanted to
hold her but she stepped back. He stepped toward her with his
arms still out. "Baby, listen."

She squeezed her eyes shut.

"Sonofabitching bastard!" she screamed. "Can't stomach the
sight of you!"

She looked around for something to snatch up, then balled
her fists and took a step toward him. "Mean to have nerve enough
to take her side? First you *had* it . . ." She flew into him screaming and pounding wherever her fists would land.

That's when all hell broke loose. Everyone jumped on him—
James, Marcus, and the Woman—cursing, screaming, kicking,
punching. James broke away and ran upstairs, then came back
down with a slat from his bed. He lifted it and it came down on
the Husband's head.

The whole room froze.

You covered your ears with your hands and screamed. The walls moved first—slow, in and out—then the table, the door, Marcus, the Woman, James. Blending and mixing, folding together like batter. Their voices blended too and you drowned them out with your screams. You just stood there and screamed, Clarissa.

And screamed . . .

They dragged you to the basement door and the lock clicked on the other side. You fell on the dark stairs. I stayed with you near the top steps, didn't want to go down there. The furnace at the bottom made me think about hell.

I tried to separate it all, what had been real and what I imagined. I felt my sides and arms and then I knew it had been real. I saw the gash in the Husband's head inside my own head. I saw him leave. I wondered if he'd die on the way to wherever he was going.

I sat still.

The door cracked and light squeezed through it. Then James squeezed through and eased the door shut. I stood up to run but he caught me by the arm and held it tight. His fingers pressed into the still sore spots.

I didn't fight, didn't say a word. He pulled me down the steps to the floor near the furnace. And he pulled your skirt up and finished what had started this morning.

The hushed noise upstairs woke me up. I turned over and stretched. My elbow hit the step and a pain went through my arm that shocked me all the way out of my sleep.

The basement step was cold.

I got up slowly and tugged at the wet skirt that stuck to my thighs. I went over to the washtub and wet a rag, then cleaned the pee off the step. Then I sat on the floor so I could lay my head on the bottom step and get warm from the furnace at the same time. I forgot about the hell inside it—the heat felt good.

A woman's voice that I had never heard before called for me to come upstairs. I looked around to make sure I wasn't in the wrong house.

I thought about last night. I listened. Just the woman's voice. I followed it into the front room.

The Husband sat quietly in the corner chair with his head between both hands, not dead like I thought he might have been but with his head wrapped up. James stood on the stairs and leaned against the wall. I looked over at the Woman—her lips smiled but her eyes didn't. Marcus just looked scared.

"Why you people never talk is beyond me," I heard the strange woman's voice say. My eyes followed it to a tall burly looking woman in a gray suit standing near the front door. She looked around the room, then shook her head and wrote something in a little brown notebook that her hands seemed too big to hold. A skinny young man with stringy brownish-yellow hair stood next to her with his arms folded. He didn't look at us or anything—his mind was on someplace else.

"I don't get it. You knock the hell out of each other and nobody sees a thing. Get killed almost and you never know one thing about it." She glanced over at me. The glance turned into a stare—first at my skirt and then at my arms, like they were reminding her about something she had forgotten. I hid them behind my back and she wrote in the little brown notebook.

"You Ellen?" the big woman asked, looking up from her notebook straight at me. Her voice was too soft for the way she looked.

I tried to make my voice soft like hers. "Yes, ma'am."

"Wanna tell me what happened last night?"

I looked from the Woman to the Husband. He didn't lift his

head. The Woman's smile was still there but her eyes were too.

I looked for the spot with the map on the linoleum again.

"Don't know."

The lady sucked in air, then let it out loudly.

"Must have been asleep," I said.

She didn't say anything, just stared hard at me for a long time like I might decide to tell her something else. No one said a word.

She moved closer, keeping her eyes on me.

"Did anyone . . . do anything to you?" She said the words carefully.

I saw last night. And I saw you. You and James. I looked over at the Husband, then back at the lady.

"No," I said. "Just fell in some bushes."

~

"For the wage of sin is death, He said. How many Deadly Sins are there?"

"Seven," we answered.

"Can anyone name them?"

"Pride, envy, gluttony . . ." someone said.

"Anger, sloth . . ."

"Covetousness . . ."

Marcus looked over at me, then raised his hand.

"Lust," he said.

"Means you're going to die," Marcus said.

"It's your *soul* that dies in hell, Marcus—you didn't hear all of it."

"All the same," he said. "And you always look down like you know you're going down there."

"Where?"

"Hell," he said.

"I confessed."

"Lust *and* covetousness, cause it was with the Husband," he went on. "Ellen, that's double."

"Wasn't *him*, I told you. Wasn't anybody."

"Saw the stuff, Ellen. Lying too—that's three."

"Lying's venial," I said to the sidewalk. "Confessed them too."

He stopped and looked at me. "What if you die before you get a chance to confess? Ever think about that?" He threw his hands up. "What is it about it that you like so much?"

"I hate it."

"And Leslie Johnson too, I saw her and James do it behind Miss Morris's. What's it feel like?"

I didn't say anything, just walked fast. He ran to catch up.

"Know that new girl, Ellen? A couple of times I thought about doing it with her." He confessed like it was a sin he should have confessed to Father.

I stopped. "Marcus!"

"Can't though," he said. "Don't want to burn in hell."

The Cila Lady came out of Mr. Julius's and turned around when she saw me. I looked around like I was searching for someone, then crossed the street.

"Young lady," she called after me. I kept walking and Marcus followed me.

"Why're you crossing here?" he asked.

"Thought it might be a shortcut," I said.

"This way?"

"Uum."

He looked at me funny. "Wasn't that the lady across the alley?"

"Didn't see."

"You know, Ellen, the one they talk about. Wasn't she calling you?"

"Uh uh. Must have been someone else."

*Mr. Julius smiled and gave the Cila Lady a flower pin. She took off her straight blue skirt and put on a tight red dress that matched her toenails. Mr. Julius kissed her.*

*She took his hand and they went to the little room behind the counter. He leaned her against the wall and took his thing out and the back of her head pounded the wall. She laughed and opened herself up. It went inside her and her head stopped pounding. He fell on the floor, burned ash gray like coal soot. Dead. And his thing turned into a snake as little as a worm. I stepped on it.*

"Don't come back here much anymore." The Cila Lady reached a handful of long weeds across to me, then tied one on the fence.

"No, ma'am. Been at all my friends' houses."

"Mean you have other friends? All you ever mentioned was that one—what's her name?"

"Clarissa."

"Yeah. Thought you were going to let me meet her."

"Forgot," I said.

"Like you keep forgetting to ask if I can do your hair," she laughed.

"Yes, ma'am."

She stopped and squinted at me and I pulled a weed knot through the fence.

"Don't have much to say about anything, do you? All I can get out of you is that Catholic stuff and your Clarissa friend. Then it's like pulling teeth." She watched me tie the next knot. "When the water is still, it runs deep," she said and waited like she had asked a question that I should have answered.

"That's what my uncle used to say," she went on. "Used to take me over near the Meramac when we lived outside Saint

Louis. Mostly to fish. Sometimes we'd go when he just wanted
to be someplace quiet, still. When the water was still he'd say
that's when it ran deep, the way he liked it. But when it rushed in
waves like it had too much to fuss about, he'd say, Too shallow—
let's go."

She waited again, then stuck her hands on her hips. "Know
why I take to you so?"

Something to do with the dream, I thought, but I said, "No,
ma'am."

"He liked his people that way. Quiet. That was his way too.
He'd have liked you. Would have put you right with still water."

I wondered if "he" was Mr. Stevens. "Did he move here?" I
asked.

"You kidding? He loved Saint Louis, stayed right there in that
raggedy old house we lived in till the day he died."

I wanted to cry for the quiet man. I don't know why, just did,
so I turned my head so she wouldn't see. But she laughed and I
laughed too—don't know why I did that either.

"I'd still be there too if they didn't give me this house in probate. Doing hair and going to school when I could make enough
to pay for it." She stopped and studied my face. "Probate's a court
where they give you something that belongs to you when someone dies," she answered the question that was on my mind. "They
took it when my father died. Two years later they said it belonged
to me, and the woman he kept had to move."

"But Mrs. Stevens was the only one who lived there," I said.

"Oh that Jessie woman. She wasn't *Mrs.* Stevens—she was his
outside woman."

Still didn't make sense.

"Thomas Stevens had only one wife—my mother. And one
child—me. Never did take care of either of us. Jessie Hawkins—
that's what her real name is—used to watch me when
Mama worked. He fooled around with Jessie back then. I was

only six but I knew they weren't just talking out in that shed.

"Then my grandfather died and my father took the insurance and bought a car one day. Took his burial money and savings the next. Then took Jessie and her kids and disappeared. Didn't even come back for the funeral. Mama had to borrow money to bury *his* father."

"Still didn't work when he lived with Mrs. Steve—Hawkins," I whispered.

"Why ain't I surprised?" she laughed.

"And he fooled around on her too," I said real quick. I hoped it would make her laugh again.

But she just said, "It all comes around," then squatted down and studied the weeds.

*Is that why he died like that?* I asked inside my head because it wouldn't come out of my mouth.

"The water's deep again," she said.

"Humh?"

"A lot of *something's* on your mind, I can tell. Got too quiet."

I tried to ask again and it stuck inside my neck. So I just pushed it out another way, and it rolled out of my mouth quick. "Is that why Mr. Julius died?"

She stopped studying the weeds and looked up at me. "Mr. who?"

It became a whisper. "Julius. The man at the store over by Field Street."

"Where I saw you last Tuesday and you acted like you didn't see me?"

I tucked my head.

"That's Mr. Julius?"

"Yes, ma'am," I whispered.

"When did that happen?"

"Last Tuesday night."

She stood up and leaned on one hip. "Well they put a bad one out this time," she laughed. "I was just there and that man's just as much living as we are." She thought for a minute. "Ever tie a love knot?" She reached three long weed blades over to me.

"No, ma'am. I'm not in love. I mean, I'm in love but he's not really my boyfriend."

"Don't need one—it's just what they call it. Put your fingers out like this." She held her fingers out to show me. "Mama died when I was about your age," she said as she tied the strands around my fingers. "Maybe a year or two younger. My Uncle Claude took me in, cared for me like his brother was supposed to have done. Passed me off as his outside child—you know how people talk when a man without a wife keeps a girl that's not his. That's how I saw myself too. Outside. He did all that he could for me—fed me, sent me to school, college. But I kept feeling outside, like I didn't quite fit."

She shook her head and let out a little laugh. "Got that feeling about being here too. People are friendly enough, I guess. They speak and wave—when I speak and wave to them. But they sure don't give me any hair business. Put up signs in all the stores and no one comes. Guess that's what happens to an outside person.

"Got that feeling about you too. Like you're an outside child, I mean. But you have people." She waited for me to answer, then shrugged her shoulders. "All this time and I don't even know your name."

"Shirley," I said real low. Then I said, "It's Shirley," out loud to the ground.

She wrinkled her nose. "Doesn't fit you," she said.

*The Cila Lady took me in her little car to see that Mr. Julius wasn't dead but was all the way down in Saint Louis on the edge of the Meramac River. Naked. The water rushed all around his legs and roared so loud it sounded like it came from inside my ears.*

*"Got to put your clothes on, Mr. Julius!" I shouted to him. But the*

*Cila Lady said he couldn't hear me unless we made the water quiet first. And she handed me a jar with a little brown rubbery knot inside it.*

*"Go over to the edge and ease it into the water," she said. "That'll make it quiet."*

*"What is it?" I asked.*

*"Mrs. Stevens's lump," she said, then pushed me toward the water where Mr. Julius was.*

*I unscrewed the lid and felt along the water's edge with my foot for a still place to put it.*

*"Hey, gal," Mr. Julius called to me and I looked over at him. "See what you did to me, gal," he said and his thing rose up.*

*I went over to him. The water scratched my ears. I opened the jar and threw Mrs. Stevens's lump on Mr. Julius.*

*The water roared louder.*

I woke up and the roar was still down inside my ear, Clarissa. This one. And it scratched and fluttered at the same time while it roared. I tilted my head, then beat my ear against the mattress but it was still there. So I got on my knees and beat my ear against the floor until it hurt, but it just went down further inside my ear. Louder. I went to school and Sister asked me why I kept making faces and moving my head around.

"It's in my ear," I said.

She grabbed my elbow and pulled me out into the hall. "*What's* in your ear?" she asked.

"Water or a lump—something."

She turned my head and looked inside. "There's nothing here," she said.

"But I *hear* it. And it moves."

"Must be a roach," she said like she knew exactly what it was.

"Laziness is a sin before God," the Woman said while the noise kept up inside my ear. "Keep being too lazy to get up, keep peeing in the bed, and He'll find a way to make you pay for it right where you lay. And why do you stay at the alley so much? Nothing out there but trash and that junk man that passes through. Is it him you keep going back there for?"

The noise fluttered faster when she said *passes*.

"No, ma'am."

"You never know. I know that's what the filthy do some-times—they do their garbage in the alley. It all goes together. Is that why you keep going back there?"

"No, ma'am."

"Then take what you're taking out and come right back. Looks bad for us, you being back there all the time. If you ain't doing nothing you won't even *want* to be there."

A lady called my name and I jumped up. She took me back to a dingy green room that smelled like old sweat and iodine. A doctor was doing something to a man behind a blue curtain. I don't know what it was but the man cussed and hollered and the doctor told him that he couldn't help him if he didn't hold still. Six or seven other people laid on skinny beds all around the room. Some talked, some just held their lips tight and shook their heads, grunting "um, um, um." Most of them stopped and looked up when I came in, like they could hear the roar inside my ear. I stared back at them like I could see what was wrong with them too. But the noise inside my ear was louder than their sickness so I looked away to a picture of a woman's inside private parts on the wall next to a gray metal table.

The doctor came from behind the curtain and wiped his hands on his long shirt while he read something on a board. "Ellen?" he asked while he motioned for me to sit in a chair next to the table. He didn't wait for me to answer, didn't say anything else. Just left and came back with a wide-bottom jar and a fat ee-through hose.

"What's in your ear?" he asked, screwing the bottom of the hose to the jar's long skinny neck.

I told him the same thing Sister told me. "Must be a roach."

He held the other end of the hose up to my ear and it sucked until the roar and fluttering stopped, and the only noise left came from the hose. He turned it off, then held the jar near my face.

"Nope, not a roach," he said. "Know what it is?"

I watched a tiny chinch bug flit around in the water inside the jar until it gave up and stopped moving.

"A knot," I said.

~

I met the new girl that Marcus is in love with. I like her too—*too* much. But I'm not in love with her, just in love with how pretty she is. I keep imagining that I'm pretty also and that she's in love with how pretty I am too. In my head I see her brushing my hair that's long and light brown like hers—not short with little plaits all over like it is now—and she puts her arm around me and tells me that I can brush hers when she's finished. We both smile about the Little Monkeyshine Boy—he's in love with her and me at the same time.

I don't think she likes me as much as I like her but she likes me some. That's good enough.

She was coming from the store when I sat out on the front steps. Can't sit on the backporch steps anymore—the Woman said it's too close to the alley. The new girl stopped and asked if I wanted her to come over. That's how I met her.

I looked around to see if there was someone else who she might have been talking to and was glad to see that she was really talking to me. I didn't say anything, she was just too pretty. She walked right up and put her bag down, then sat next to me on the same step.

I opened my mouth and a funny voice squeaked out. "Wanna sit next to me," it said, like she wasn't already sitting there.

She laughed at the way it sounded. She *smelled* pretty too, like soap.

"I'm Madeline," she said staring at my arms.

"Um hum." I kept on smelling her but I pretended that I wasn't.

"Ain't you going to tell me your name?"

"Tamajrah," I said. I hoped she might think the name was pretty. *God must really love her.*

She wrinkled her nose just like the Cila Lady does. "Tomorrow?"

"No, Ta-mar-*ah!*" I said, then made up the letters as I spelled it. "T-a-m-a-j-r-a-h. Ta-mar-*ah*, not like tomorr-*ow*."

She wrinkled her nose again. "Spelled with a *j?*"

"It's silent."

"But why does it have one? Doesn't belong in it," she said.

"It needs something silent." I guess I thought about a silent letter because I like silence. It's like opening the window at night when everyone's asleep. It's so quiet then that I can hear the wind touch my face and sing me to sleep. The silence feels so safe it has to be Glue. *J* must be silent because it stands for *just—* just silent.

"Figures," she said.

"Humh?"

"Tomorrow. Name like that would fit a Peculiar."

"A Peculiar?"

"That's what Daddy said you are. Saw you sitting here the day we moved in. Said you had such a good time talking and laughing and it wasn't another soul in sight. Daddy said, Now, that's a Peculiar if I ever saw one." She stared at me like she was trying to figure out what else a Peculiar might do, then tucked her head and whispered, "I saw you too."

"Was talking to a cat—it was in the bushes," I said.

She stared down at my arms again and frowned. "What's the matter with'm?"

They were so ugly next to hers. The welts were still there. The old ones at least were turning brown and disappearing. But the new ones looked like red streaks and the raised hieroglyphics that we learned about last year, like they were telling all our secrets. I eased both arms behind my back and sat on my hands to make sure they wouldn't come out and show themselves again.

"Fell in the bushes looking for the cat," I said.

She scrunched her nose. "You smell like pee."

"It must've peed on me," I said.

I heard the Woman upstairs at the front door.

"Who you here to see?" I heard her ask. Then she said, "Don't know no *Tomorrow*."

My insides knotted.

"Ellen's who you must be talking about," she said. "Honey, she ain't having no company. What made you to come looking for her in the first place?"

I tried to make my insides untie themselves.

"Well then, honey, you ain't found out about her. You'll find out soon enough—ask anybody. Half the time she don't know *who* she is, you can see that already—calling herself *Tomorrow* like that's a name anyway. Whoever heard of somebody naming a child *Tomorrow?*"

I listened to her tell Madeline everything I had hoped she wouldn't find out.

". . . and she pisses in the bed too," the Woman went on. "A big old stinking girl like her, just like a baby. Stinks the whole house up so, you want to kill her . . ."

I listened to the door close and watched Madeline walk away. I called her back in my head, told her that she had just imagined the Woman said those things. But she kept walking.

I turned to wring the clothes when I heard the Woman coming down the stairs.

"Why'd you tell her she could come see you?" she said to my back.

I turned around. Her eyes were red.

"I didn't," I said.

"Well *some*body must've and the only one it could've been was you," she said. "Look at me, Ellen, better hear this good. Don't let me hear about you going and telling *no*body they can come see you. You understand me?"

"Yes, ma'am."

"And don't let me hear tell of you going and asking to go *see* nobody or I'll rip your goddamn crazy head off!"

She threw the jar of beets that she was taking to the cellar. It shattered against the wall behind me.

"Now clean it up!"

She started back up the stairs but got halfway up, then turned and sat down on them. "Don't need to be playing," she mumbled. "Ain't nothing but dogs out there and you know it cause you been wallowing with one." She shook her head. "And got the nerve to want to play."

Beet juice was spattered all over the wall, the floor, and all over my dress. I picked up the broken glass. It stained my fingers as red as the spot on the wall. Blood. I thought about the Curse, about the baby I'd flushed, and James. Womanness and the Root Worker and sin. *Three in one, and one in three*—the Blessed Trinity song. I changed my thought back to the Woman just in case it would offend God and cause Him to send me straight to hell.

". . . brought her smell back with him and laid it right in my bed," the Woman said to nobody but herself. "Just *brought* it to me. Didn't think you'd know, he said like I hadn't laid down and had these kids by him. Must think I'm somebody dumb."

She looked all around the basement, then went on talking to herself.

"Tramp's ugly as hell, they said. Ain't clean worth a damn, lays up with everything that comes her way, and he *still* goes over there sniffing up under it."

She looked up at me like I had popped in out of nowhere, with a look like something had just happened that made her feel sorry for me. "Sniffed up under you too, baby," she said to me sadly. "Know you ill-aformed, but sniffed just the same."

She straightened her shoulders and stared off at nothing.

"Sniffing up under *her* again." Her voice rose. "Could've at least got something better, wouldn't have been so bad. Ought to leave him for it. Ought to pick up right now and leave him with all of'm just like you left us."

Then, like she was answering something that I had said to her, she said to me, "But I can't leave these kids. What else can I do with'm except stay? Don't you see, Mama? Can't say I don't need him, it'd be a lie."

She stood and stretched, then sat back down again.

"All I can do is put down something to keep him here. All the stuff in the world won't keep him from sniffing though."

I eased over to the steps and sat on the one beneath her feet. I thought I should say something to her but I didn't know what to say. So I just rested my chin on my knees and listened.

"Men. They're all like dogs," she said to nobody again. "They can smell it every time it's ripe, can tell before we do cause they can smell it." She stood up and shook her head. "Just like dogs in heat," she said. "Don't care what it looks like, if it's ill-aformed. If they smell it they want it."

It's been going on two months now and James hasn't bothered us. That's because I like it, Clarissa. I used to scrub myself, raw almost, ever since the Woman told me about the ripeness smell that makes them want it. Used to scrub every Saturday and he'd do it anyway. And I'd rush to Confession before Mass and pray to God to forgive me for all that sin.

I got tired and gave up, didn't care about sin and hell, just gave up and let James do what he wanted. That's when it started to feel good. As soon as he knew I liked it he didn't want it anymore.

Fighting, I guess, makes it ripe.

~

I miss the Cila Lady.

I saw her in her yard when I made a fire to burn my womanhood rag. She looked up and saw me and called, "Hi, Shirley." I acted like I didn't hear her and threw the rag in the fire, then ran back to the house and closed the door. Seemed like she would have seen me inside the house from the alley.

She has a boyfriend now, I heard the Woman tell Aunt Della. She said she heard he's one of the preachers from Tabernacle.

"Tabernacle?" Aunt Della looked at the Woman like she didn't believe what she heard. "You said *Tabernacle?*"

"Ain't that what it sounded like I said?" the Woman answered.

"The over-on-*Chene*-Street Tabernacle?"

"You know of another one?"

"But Tabernacle's *Apostolic*," Aunt Della told the Woman. "How'd she get herself an *Apostolic* one?"

"Been going there ever since she came up here, I heard." The Woman was proud that she could tell Aunt Della something for a change. "For some months now. *And* she works for the county. Got a good office job, I heard. Two-something a hour."

"Almost good as in the plant. I thought she did hair."

"Does that too—supposed to have been good back where she came from, I heard. Charged too much, but good. They say she works with figures too."

"Must be educated," Aunt Della said. ". . . *Apostolic*. Then the old woman didn't know what she was talking about."

The Woman knew that Aunt Della had figured something out so she just sat down and waited, then said, "Okay, Della, what'd you come up with this time?"

"That woman can't be one of those things you said she was, what was it?"

"Cila."

"She can't be cause Apostolics don't take to that kind of stuff—it's devil's work. If somebody among them just *thinks* about it they have a way of knowing. And can't get near one of those Apostolic preachers—they'd drive one clear off the earth."

"She still ain't no saint," the Woman frowned. "He ain't either, preacher or not. He was at her house all night more than a few times, and supposed to be a man of God."

"He's a man just the same," Aunt Della said.

"And they ain't married, so it ain't no excuse except that, educated or not, she's just another whore and he's gonna sniff and get just like any other man . . . Ellen, stop listening to grownfolk's talk and get my cigarettes . . ."

I liked her when I thought she was a cila lady. Now it seems like she's just a plain lady who must be smart. I still call her the Cila Lady though. I don't know any other name for her. And I still take her combs out and act like they can do something too. Not as much since James has left us alone.

I thought about her smelling ripe and I didn't want to see her. I thought about her boyfriend too, smelling her, then emptying himself in her like James did to me. And I hated her.

The Woman's nice all the time now and it's just like Glue. She doesn't have much to say to any of us, especially the Husband. All she says to him most of the time is, "Honey, how you feeling?"

and "You want something to eat?" The Husband doesn't know what to make of the way she's been acting. I don't either.

She spends most of the time cooking and cleaning and leaving me alone, mostly cooking. And she hums and sings about how the stars don't come out since she left her man behind and how a good for nothing man can bring a woman down. After that she sings a "Jesus, set me free" song louder than the others.

She sings the "Left my man behind" and "Jesus, set me free" songs when she works. It seems to make her do everything harder. Presses the iron down harder, clangs the pans harder and louder. And I think about her loving the man back where she came from and being like a mule again.

The Woman does most of my work too. Won't even let me help most of the time. She takes whatever I'm doing away and says, "Go on outside. Don't nobody appreciate me no way."

She caught me sneaking down the street to jump rope with Madeline yesterday. Marcus told me. But she didn't say anything about it, didn't do anything either. She just watched, Marcus said, then went right back to humming and singing and ironing.

So I sneaked out and jumped rope with Madeline again this morning.

~

The Woman came back from seeing the Root Worker. I had a feeling we might be in trouble so I stayed upstairs and listened to her scream and curse the Husband and his girlfriend to nobody but herself. She called me and I eased the bedroom door open a little but I didn't answer. I heard her go from room to room, still cursing. She stopped, then went to the stairs and started again.

"Just been too damn long," she said. "Just too long for anybody to take all this hurting and carrying on." She called up the stairs, "Ellen!"

I didn't move.

"Gonna fix him, that low-down dog of a man, fix'm both . . ."

She mumbled something. I couldn't hear much of it except something about killing herself while everyone else was killing her too.

"It's all gonna end right here, this day," she said out loud.

I heard her walk away, then call out the back door, "Ellen!"

My heart thumped so loud I thought she might hear it and come after me. I held my breath and waited.

"Won't come to no good," I heard her say right outside the bedroom door and I jumped straight up. The door opened all the way and she stood so close to me I felt her breath.

"Put your shoes on," she said. Just that. "Put your shoes on," like she hadn't been cursing and hollering and calling me, and I didn't answer.

The Woman took me with her to see the lady who's supposed to be the Husband's girlfriend. She lives on a street where the sun doesn't shine much and most of the houses are boarded up. Those that aren't boarded up have windows that are so full of soot you can draw pictures on them with just your fingers. The Woman said the soot comes from the factory where the Husband works now.

"This is that woman he goes to sniffing up under when he gets off from work," the Woman said to me on the way over.

She stopped the car in front of a grayish looking house that wasn't boarded up but looked like it should have been. I don't know what color it really was, the soot was so thick on it. All of the houses were covered with soot.

Hunks of gray speckled dirt and big chunky pieces of crumbled concrete were piled in front of the porch where steps should have been. And the house sort of leaned to one side like it wanted to just roll over and take a nap against the boarded-up store next to it.

Dirty curtains, as tired and gray looking as the house, flapped from the open windows that still had glass. The other windows had wrinkled up old cardboard shoved in them.

"Black as tar, ugly as sin, and fat as all hell," the Woman said. "Got a house full of little whiny nappyheads too, running all over the place and hanging to her skirt tail. Not a one got the same daddy, I heard. Ain't got a pot to piss in on top of all that. Sleeping on the floor and carrying on." She shook her head in disgust. "And got the nerve to be going with somebody and making some more babies. I keep saying it, a man don't care just as long as he can smell it. Now you can see it for yourself."

The Girlfriend was wide and blue-black with hair as short and nappy as ours. She had a thousand of those little Medusa plaits on her head too and a big long dirty green skirt over hips that sort of squished around when she walked. I had never seen a grown woman with dinky plaits before, except for the women in those pictures of Africa.

She held a little new baby in one arm and it sucked on her breast. Two little dirty kids who both looked to be the same age— about two or three—held on to her skirt. They looked the same way I imagine all of my kids will look every time I think about what the Woman said about me being able to get pregnant again. Only my kids won't be ugly because their daddy'll be cute like the Little Monkeyshine Boy.

The Woman said that the new baby is the Husband's. She said she thinks the two smallest ones might be his too because they look a lot like him. She's not sure about the little girl who's about four or five though. Said it's hard to tell because she looks too much like the Girlfriend.

The Woman asked the Girlfriend where did she and the Husband lay since there wasn't anywhere to sit, much less do it. The Girlfriend stared at her, then turned her back.

The Woman bit her lip. "Where did he lay with you?" she

asked again just like she had asked me *Who layed with you, Ellen?* I watched the baby suck on the Girlfriend's breast and it didn't seem like a breast anymore but like a long stretched-out tittie. And it hanged down like it had been sucked and pulled on for a long time. I thought about Mr. Julius feeling on mine and imagined the Husband sucking and pulling on the Girlfriend's tittie just like the baby did.

The Girlfriend wrinkled her forehead and looked like she was starting to get a headache. She handed the baby to one of the little girls and took the Woman to a room off the kitchen that opened onto the backporch. The Woman called to me to come back there with them and said she wanted me to see what the Husband had been doing since I was so crazy about him.

The room was stark naked empty.

"Where did he lay with you?" the Woman asked again.

The Girlfriend pointed at the floor. "There," she said and looked away.

The Woman laughed and the Girlfriend looked right at me. Her eyes filled up.

I didn't know what to do, just felt as if I had been right in that little room watching when they did it. Knew I had to get away from there. So I concentrated on the tiny hole in the old cardboard in the window, making myself small enough to squeeze through it and leave the room.

The Woman's mad.

Knowing that the Girlfriend is blue-black is worse for her than finding out that the Husband had been with her. Aunt Della told her that it's yellow women he likes to look at so whatever the Girlfriend has it must be good. The Woman told her to go to hell and cursed her so, she had to leave. *Good!* I said. But I didn't say it out loud.

The Woman and the Girlfriend call each other all the time now, cussing at each other and talking about kicking each other's asses. It got worse when the Girlfriend called the Woman and told her that she hadn't seen the Husband in more than two weeks and she needed milk and bread for her kids.

The Woman asked her what did she expect her to do and if she thought she was some kind of a fool. The Girlfriend told her that she was just as much to blame for her kids being hungry as the Husband is because she won't let him leave.

What did she say that for?

The Woman went into all kinds of fits and cursed the Girlfriend to everything she could think of.

"Black ugly ink-spitting stinking-assed bitch!" she finally screamed. "You think your stuff's that good, come and get him now!" and she banged the phone down and told me to go get her cigarettes. I should have known that she was ready to kill anything that came near her but I thought about it too late. As soon as I handed the cigarettes to her she kicked me. And she screamed and cursed me and everyone else who she said were the whores and bitches who made her life hell.

The Root Worker sat with her eyes shut while the Woman told her about the Girlfriend. I thought she was asleep. I think the Woman must have thought so too. She stopped in the middle of the part about the Girlfriend saying that she was to blame for her kids being hungry and stood up. The Root Worker opened her eyes just a little and said, "Shush!" The Woman sat back down and waited. I sat still like the Root Worker and listened to her breathe heavy in the half dark room.

Someone said something. I didn't hear them but the Root Worker answered, "Yes!"

I opened my eyes and didn't see anyone. The Root Worker's eyes were still closed but her lips trembled.

They must not have heard her. She threw up her arms all of a sudden and shouted, "Yes, I said!"

And then she was still again.

Half the night seemed to go by. I fell asleep and woke up and she still sat like that. Eyes closed, lips trembling. The Woman watched her, still waiting. I straightened myself up in the chair and watched too.

The Root Worker finally got up and went to the other side of the blanket curtain. She didn't say anything, just left like we weren't sitting there. She came back and sat a big box that said EGGS on the floor in front of the Woman.

"Put nine of'm in here," she said handing her a brownish pillowcase.

The Woman pulled short fat red candles out of the box and counted them, then laid them carefully in the pillowcase.

"When you get home I want you to write his name on each one three times," the Root Worker told her. She handed the Woman a little jar. "Rub some of this on all of'm when you get through," she said. "Then I want you to do this exactly like I say. Write his name three times on a big piece of paper and dig a wide hole six inches deep on the left side of your yard." She nodded toward me. "Get her to help you dig. Put the paper in the hole, then go get a dirty sock of his and his hat. Cut a piece of the inside of his hat and lay it in the hole on top of the paper." She studied the Woman. "Light one of these candles and set it all on fire. Then I want you to go get a glass of water and put some of this in the water." She crumpled a dried up leaf into a little packet, then rubbed it under her breast and gave it to the Woman.

"Put another one of these candles in the hole and burn it for one hour exactly and say his name one time every twenty minutes. Cover the hole with what you burn your rags in and set the glass next to the drum.

"Do it at midnight tomorrow," she said. "That's important. Put another one there at six the next night and burn it an hour too. Say his name like you did with the first one. Then at every six and midnight after that till they've all been lit."

The Woman put the jar and packet in the pillowcase with the candles and we got up to leave.

The Root Worker followed us down the stairs. "Take that woman the bread and milk that she asked for. Do it on the morning right after the last midnight." When we reached the sidewalk she said, "And this is what else you need to do." She pulled the Woman to the side and whispered.

The Girlfriend didn't open the door when she saw that it was us on her porch. The Woman hollered through the screen that she had prayed over it and God told her to take the food to the kids because they don't have a thing to do with what goes on between grown folks. The Girlfriend opened the door, took the bag of food from me, then turned and walked back into the house. She hollered over her shoulder that we could come in.

The Woman picked one of the little girls up and looked around for a place to sit. She gave up and sat on the floor when she saw that the two boys who sat in the only chair wouldn't get up to let her sit down. I just stood and looked around the room for another window with cardboard that I could squeeze through. I didn't see one so I watched the boys bounce their little jack balls in front of the chair.

The Woman asked the Girlfriend how long had she known the Husband and which of the kids were his. The Girlfriend said she had met him around six or seven years ago, and the baby was his and so was the one that the Woman held in her lap.

"Sure that's all?" the Woman asked like the Girlfriend might have forgotten something. "Funny, that other one looks just like him and the little girl's young enough to be about the age that going with him six or seven years'd make him the daddy."

The Girlfriend told her that the other two were by someone else and she knew because she didn't go with the Husband until she found out he was leaving the Woman. When she said that I stopped watching the boys and looked over at the Woman.

She sat the little girl down on the floor, then bit her lip and stood up. "Who told you that?"

"He did," the Girlfriend answered matter of factly. "Said he was leaving you first chance he could get."

I thought the Woman would hit her but she laughed and said, "Funny, it's my first hearing and he told me just last week he wants to buy me a new car and he'll keep the old one."

The Girlfriend frowned. "Well he told *me* he was leaving you," she said. "Said he ain't had you no more since he got with me. And he don't want you no more cause all he keeps thinking about is what *we* got—he *ain't* laying with you, is he?"

The Woman laughed. "Damn right he ain't," she said. "And it ain't cause he don't want it. He's pussy whipped. All he does is beg me for it every time he can. Got nerve enough to try and pay me for it when I tell him no." She twisted her lips into a frown. "Can't *pay* me to lay with him." She stared at the Girlfriend, then shook her head slowly. "Honey, he ain't going nowhere," she said. "Not with you. Not with nobody."

"He gives *me* money," the Girlfriend said. "And I take it too. All the time—be a fool not to. He tells me it's worth gold to him."

The Woman laughed loud at the Girlfriend. "I don't care if it's *made* out of gold," she said. "And if it backs up on his brain so he can't even see straight, he still ain't never gonna leave me."

It seemed like when the Woman told the Girlfriend that, the whole thing ended. They didn't talk about the Husband anymore but talked about kids and clothes and how sick they had been at times, just like they were friends. The Woman told the Girlfriend about Aunt Della's growing hands and said that she ought to let her do her hair to make it grow.

The Woman told the Root Worker about what had happened,

including what the Girlfriend said about which kids were the Husband's.

"Oh, yeah," she said when she stood up to leave. She handed the Root Worker a bag that she held with its top rolled down tight the whole time we were there. "Got the drawers. Stole'm out of her bathroom."

The Husband stays in bed most of the time.

He won't come downstairs much anymore except to go to work and to go to Mass. Then he comes straight home and goes right back to bed. He won't talk much either and won't eat any food that the Woman cooks. He's scared the Root Worker might have given her something to put in it. He looks like he doesn't care about anything, like all of everything's been drained out of him. The Woman says he's brooding over the Girlfriend but the Root Worker told her that love's the farthest thing from his mind. What she did with those drawers took care of that. She said he's like that because the Girlfriend's worked something on him too.

The Woman pulled out her titties when he came downstairs this morning. She stood in front of him holding both of them in her hands and asked him if he wanted them. He said, "Yeah, baby, course I do," so quietly I almost didn't hear him. But he didn't try to touch them or anything, didn't even sound like he meant it. The Woman just laughed, put them back in, and told him to go get his woman's if he can. Then she pulled her dress up and shook her naked butt, right in front of Marcus and me. Marcus turned his head to keep from seeing it but I stared with my mouth wide open.

The Husband just stood there and looked at her.

It's quiet.

James and Marcus are out in the garage, nobody here but you

and me. The Husband's at work and the Woman went somewhere, I don't know.

I imagined a lot this morning. That the Woman found out she
had only dreamed she had carried me all those months like she
thought she had. So she didn't hurt because of me. I didn't pee in
the bed because I could feel when I had to go and could wake up
before it came out.

I did wake up last night and couldn't believe it. I felt it and I
went to the bathroom. I thought I had been dreaming this morning but I felt the bed and it was dry. I told the Woman. I thought
it might make her happy but she didn't think too much of it, just
said, "I don't know what you're so excited about, should've been
doing that for the past ten years."

I'm still excited about it.

The Woman cut off all her hair last night. It's almost as short
as mine and she doesn't look as pretty as she did before she cut it.
She told the Husband that she cut it all off because she wanted it
to be short like the Girlfriend's and mine, since women with short
nappy hair seem to have more of a hold on him than she does. But
it made her sad not having much hair.

She said that a woman's hair is her crown and glory, then
looked at all the hair that had fallen into her lap and laughed to
herself.

"Ain't got no more glory," she said. "Ain't got shit."

She still shakes her butt at the Husband every now and then and
teases him with her titties, but we've gotten used to seeing her do
that now. The Husband still won't do anything. Most of the time I
forget he's even in the house he's so quiet. This morning I heard the
Woman ask him why he had to have the Girlfriend and how did it
feel to lay with somebody that ugly. He didn't answer, he never does.
But she still asks—all the time, same thing over and over. And he
keeps giving the same answer—none. Once he did say, "You know it
was you I always loved but what was I supposed to do?"

She called him everything but a child of God and he didn't say anything else.

Almost every day is Glue. The Woman stays busy cursing about the Girlfriend, talking on the phone about her, or going to the Root Worker's. She takes me with her sometimes, says she needs me there. I still hate going, especially now because I have to let her husband feel on me when the Woman doesn't have enough money to pay her. When he first felt on me it made the Woman mad, but the Root Worker told her it's natural for spirits to move through young girls and stir up the spirits inside some men to do things. She said that they should just let what happens take its course.

And things happen most of the time, it seems, when the Woman doesn't have much money. It bothered me at first but not anymore, doesn't hurt or anything. I keep imagining that I'm a cila lady when he does it. And I wait for him to turn into coal soot like Mr. Julius did in my dream. The only time it makes me feel sort of sad is when I see the Girlfriend in my head. Then I think I'm her.

The Husband goes to Mass every Sunday by himself now.

The first day, I went over to sit with him. He said he needed to be alone. Ever since, he's been sitting by himself a few pews away where I can see him. A lady asked me why I don't go over and sit with him and I told her I can't because he has to leave in a hurry as soon as Mass is over.

The Woman said that he goes to Mass just so people will notice him and think he's changed. But I don't think he goes because of what people think. He went to Confession last week and he takes Communion too. It scares me sometimes. Aunt Della said that her brother-in-law did almost the same thing before he went off and dropped dead.

Last Sunday the Woman asked the Husband if he'd ever read the part in the Bible that talks about men who forsake their wives and children to lay down with wicked women, and the part about how much God said that sinners have to suffer. He didn't answer, just put on his hat and started out the door. The Woman ran to the door after him.

"Means you gonna suffer something awful!" she yelled. "All the holiness and praying in the world ain't gonna mean a thing— you still got to suffer and pay for what you did."

The Husband came back from Mass and stood near the front door. He said, "Jesus said, Let he who ain't never sinned cast a stone," out loud so that the Woman could hear him from in the kitchen. "Said that right here in the Bible." He didn't say another word, just took off his hat and went upstairs back to bed.

That's what started the holy war. Not the real Holy War but what I call the holy war because the Woman and the Husband keep looking for passages in the Bible to prove they're right.

The Woman told the Husband to leave the other day and he told her he couldn't. Then he pulled out his Bible and read her the "let no man put asunder" passage and said they'd both burn in hell if she put him out, and said he could find that in the Bible too.

"I don't know what you so worried about then," the Woman said to him, "cause, baby, *this* is hell!"

It's been hell for me and Marcus too. The Woman keeps stopping us from what we're doing to make us look for passages to write down. I thought it might be a sin so I wrote, "Waste not, want not," "Four score and seven years," and "Give me liberty." The Woman said that I'm too stupid to even do that right.

There's candles and stuff all over the house—voodoo candles and blessed candles, holy water and voodoo oil. The Husband brings the holy ones from the church, and the Woman brings the voodoo ones from the Root Worker's. They use them against each other, holy power against voodoo power. And they steal from each other whichever candle or oil they believe will give them the most power against the others. They get mad at each other over it too. Fighting mad. One day the Husband stole a candle from the Woman and burned it. When she found out what he had done she went at him.

I hate going to Mass now almost as much as I hate going to the Root Worker's. I hate seeing the Husband there. I hate the sermons, the altar. Most of all I hate the candles. I hate the novenas, the devotions, indulgences for the souls in purgatory—all of the candles.

I dream about candles all the time. I dream about candles and babies with no faces, candles and fighting, candles and cursing, screaming, root working. Candles and men feeling on me, candles and blood—candles and hell.

I burned all of it.

I burned the candles and I burned the oil and root powder and the Bibles. I put them in two big grocery bags and took them outside, made a fire in the oildrum, and watched them burn.

The fire crackled and spit and the glass popped. I watched the bags fold away into soot. And the wax from the holy candles and the voodoo candles melted together until I couldn't tell which was pagan and which was holy.

More glass popped and the Bible pages singed to dust that looked like root powder. The oil whined and the wax flowed. It reminded me of souls crying in purgatory, spirits crying.

I wanted it to burn faster so that it would all end before the Woman and the Husband came home. But after a while I didn't care what happened as long as it was gone.

I watched it—hell and purgatory. Sins and martyrs. Spirits, roots, fixes, souls. Charity, Long Suffering—I watched it burn until the fire burned out and there was nothing left but ashes and scorched broken glass.

The Husband stopped going to Mass.

The Woman told Aunt Della that she didn't know why he had even bothered to go in the first place since the church is full of devils. She said that I'm the biggest one and the Husband's the next.

I'm not really sure why he stopped but ever since I burned the candles and stuff he seemed to not want to go anymore. First he'd get there late and would look around like he was either lost or in the wrong place. Two Sundays after that he didn't take Communion. Finally he just stopped going altogether. He doesn't bring any more candles home either. He won't even *look* at a candle. But he still plants roots with the Woman.

The Woman still buys candles and the Root Worker gave her something to put down to keep me from burning them up. I don't know what it is—she hides it from me. I don't want to burn anything else anyway.

The Root Worker told the Woman that I burned all the candles and Bibles because I'm full of devils and it's them inside me that wants to burn up her spirit. She said she knew that for a long time, just had hoped they might leave on their own.

"But it don't worry me none," she told the Woman when she told her about what had made me do what I did. "What I got is stronger than the devils and it'll work'm out of her but it'll cost plenty."

The Woman pays her and she works on me. Twice a week now I follow the Woman up those long steps. I watch the Root Worker mix powder with some cooked stuff that smells like cod liver oil. She mixes it with whatever else she can get her hands on—mud, pee, sometimes I don't know what it is. I drink it each time—I don't fight anymore—and it tastes different each time, but always nasty. I listen to her words that I never understand but I know that the words are mad, fighting. They *sound* mad and fighting. Always fighting.

I listen until the whole room and everything in it becomes as mixed up as the words that the Root Worker says sometimes, hums sometimes, until I'm dizzy, heavy. Then she mixes a paste of some sort and she spreads it over my naked belly while I'm still sitting there. The paste is hot. And I ask myself every time, *How can my belly be naked*, because I don't understand. All of my clothes are still on.

Last Friday I started shaking and couldn't stop when she did it. The whole room shook too. I tried to hold on to the chair to keep from falling out of it but my hands couldn't feel. I couldn't even feel my fingers. My legs and belly drew up into my neck and tied into a knot so tight I thought I was going to die. I tried to tell them but my mouth wouldn't open, so I didn't say anything. Just felt my knotted up body try to choke itself to death.

You slipped out of the chair and onto the floor and shook, Clarissa. And I watched the Root Worker reach down and pull a snake out of your belly.

I don't know when the Root Worker will finish working the devils out of me but it seems like it's going to take forever. I know the Woman's paying her a lot. She told Aunt Della that it takes almost every penny she can get her hands on. Aunt Della told her she didn't need to keep paying the Root Worker, that she'll take all of her money and won't finish until there's nothing left to get.

"All you gotta do is give me just some of that money," Aunt Della said, "and I'll beat all the devils out of her and some sense in."

The Woman acted like she didn't hear her.

Marcus still can't believe I had enough nerve to burn the Bibles. He said that he was tired of the candles and the carrying on too but he wouldn't burn Bibles up.

I did it to keep from burning the whole house down like I wanted to do, I told him.

He just stared at me for a while, then said, "Maybe you *do* have some devils in you."

He's been staying away from me most of the time since I told him that. It's just as well. He's been getting mad at me more and I don't like getting into so many fights with him.

I do feel bad about burning the Bibles—that was a sacrilege. I haven't been to Confession. I don't want to confess about the Bibles and the holy candles or about the thoughts I had about the novenas and saints and the souls in purgatory. Most of all I don't want to confess about what happens at the Root Worker's.

Sometimes when Father turns to face us at Mass I think he's turning around and looking straight at me, that he's looking at me and asking, "Don't you have something to confess?"

How can I confess? I can't say to him: *Bless me, Father, for I have burned up Bibles and blessed candles and thought they were the same as voodoo candles and pagan things. And Father, to hell with the souls in purgatory, and to hell with hell too.*

And so what about my soul, Clarissa? I think I'm going to hell anyway.

*The Root Worker tried to catch me so that she could finish work-ing all of the devils out of me before I could make it to Mass. Mass was Glue and I couldn't let her work the devils out before I got there. If she did they would have taken my soul over and turned me into one of them. I would have burned in hell with them. I made it to Mass but as soon as I got inside the door everyone got out of their pews and began to pull the devils out of me themselves. They did it the same way that the Woman and Aunt Della had pulled the baby out. It hurt the same way too, and I cried. Father came over and looked down at me. He told me that the devils had to come out or I'd burn in hell and that it wouldn't have hurt so bad if I had confessed. So I started confessing. Right in front of all of the people. They laughed and kept pulling . . .*

I went to Confession this morning and confessed everything as fast as I could. When I finished Father didn't say anything. He didn't ask me why I committed the sins or even if I was sorry for what I had done. I thought he was asleep and got ready to leave but he finally told me to say six Our Fathers and ten Hail Marys and make a good Act of Contrition.

It rained all night.

I stayed awake and listened to the thunder and lightning and the sirens. Every time there's a storm someone's house burns around here.

The Woman came into my room and said it storms because the devils are so busy that God sends the lightning to strike the wicked and burn their souls. "The wicked know who they are," she said. "They might *think* God don't know, but soon enough He strikes'm."

I prayed.

I saw a girl who looks just like me, plaits and all. Only she's a little darker than I am and has a burn on the side of her face. The Woman said the girl might be my sister.

The Woman told Aunt Della this morning that she heard the Girlfriend had an operation. She wondered how she was doing, she said, and thought she might take some things to her because she felt sorry for her being over there with all those little kids and no man. Aunt Della told her that she was full of shit.

When we got to the Girlfriend's house one of the boys came to the door and told the Woman she wasn't there. The Woman pushed the door open and we went inside anyway. That's when I saw the girl. She sat on the floor in a corner by the window plaiting one of the little girl's hair. The Woman saw her and almost dropped her purse. She stared at the girl with her mouth wide open. I tried not to stare at her like the Woman did but seeing her was too much like looking in the mirror.

The Woman asked the girl her name and she told her something. I don't remember what it was, just remember looking at her. Her eyes stayed on the girl for a long time and the girl stared right back at her. I was scared that the Woman might slap her for staring back but she just told the girl to get her an ashtray.

The girl said they didn't have one.

"Well go get me a plate or a bottle top—something," the Woman said.

The girl looked the Woman up and down, then got up and walked slowly into the kitchen looking back at the Woman. The Woman bit her lip and frowned like she was ready to slap the slow walk off her.

"Evil bitch," she mumbled to herself. "Just like your mammy."

The Girlfriend came in with the baby and a big cloth bag full of clothes and one of the little girls hanging onto her skirt tail. Her eyes got big when she saw us. "He ain't been here," she said to the Woman.

"Heard about the operation you had, thought I'd come see how you were doing. Ain't seen that one before," she said nodding toward the girl who looked like me. "Yours?"

The Girlfriend nodded and sat the bag of clothes down on the floor.

"Got that burn," the Woman said, sounding worried. "How'd it happen?"

"Burned herself with the straightening comb," the Girlfriend answered. "Five, six weeks ago. Just about all healed up now."

The Woman scratched her chin and smiled and nodded to herself like she had just found something out. "Funny. That's the same time Ellen here went off and burned all of me and my husband's stuff."

I thought about the Bibles and candles and wondered if what I had done had something to do with the girl's burn.

"*All* your stuff?" the Girlfriend asked like she couldn't believe I did it.

"Yeah, honey. Everything that meant something. Didn't know what she was doing though. Most times Ellen just ain't at herself." She nodded toward the girl again. "Must be a big help with all these kids. About how old is she? Twelve, thirteen?"

"Twelve." The Girlfriend sounded like she was tired of all the questions. "Turned twelve the seventh of March."

"Um hum." The Woman bit her lip and thought. "How long you say you knew my husband?"

"Six, seven years." The question upset the Girlfriend. "Told you that before. Could be a little bit longer, I don't know—ain't sure the exact years. Just talking about it give me a headache."

The Woman kept thinking.

"Well, honey, you just better lay down," she said to the Girlfriend. "Had that operation and all. Let me use your bathroom."

# HAINTS AND
# ILL-AFORMITY

"I SEE THE WATER'S BUSY," THE CILA LADY SAID. SHE WRINKLED her eyebrows and stared through me. "Troubled."

I scrunched my shoulders and squeezed past her and the counter. She put her groceries down and followed me out of the store.

"I'll take you home," she said.

"Can't . . ."

She took one of my bags from my arms. "Then I'll walk with you, Shirley. You need to talk to me."

*I don't want you to call me Shirley anymore.*

"You take the trash out and run back like something's after you. What's the matter?"

"Nothing."

"It's me that you're running from."

"No, ma'am. Just have to hurry up. My friends . . ."

"I've watched you for a long time," she stopped me. "Never did see *all* your friends. Not one. Don't have any, do you?"

She waited for the nothing that she knew I would say.

"Except me. And you hide from me like you hide that worry you carry around. Thought you hid it, didn't you?"

"I have to go," I said trying to take the bag. She pulled it back.

"You had a baby, Shirley," she said. "A little while back—your daddy's. Thought that was hid too."

It poured out of her mouth into me, then curled around my stomach and glued it to the sidewalk.

"Thought it was hid. But I heard them say it—Been like that ever since she had her daddy's baby—and I knew it was you they were talking about. What happened to the baby, Shirley?"

I hated her, Clarissa. Hated her polished toenails and crokono hair and her name for me that I gave her. It filled up inside me until I shut my eyes and burst.

"Don't *call* me that!"

"Don't call you *what?*" she asked.

I snatched the bag and ran.

~

I wore a soft white thing to Mass this morning. On my head. Can't count that as Peculiar though because I didn't know what it was for. The Woman keeps a box of them on the top shelf in the hall closet. When she sent me to get them from the closet, I took one out of the box to look at and feel. They're so soft and pretty.

I couldn't find my beanie so I sneaked one of them under my blouse. When no one was around I pulled it out and pinned it to my hair, then strutted to Mass just like I was Miss It. I walked straight to the front pew and genuflected slowly so that someone would notice the thing on my head and tell everyone about it.

I looked around and saw some kids elbow each other and they pointed at me. Pretty soon a lot of them were laughing. Sister didn't think it was a bit funny. Her face turned as red as a beet. She snatched it off my head, pulled me into the hallway, and gave me a big slap, saying "How dare you desecrate this church!"

I stayed in at recess and watched Sister until I thought it

might be safe to ask her how wearing something like that would desecrate a church. She said she couldn't believe I didn't know. "For Pete's sake, it's a sanitary napkin, Ellen!" she said.

*Sanitary napkin?* I looked at her.

Then she shook her head like she didn't believe how I could be *me*, period. "You don't know what it is, do you?" She sat down in the seat next to mine and said, "You use them for your monthly, Ellen."

"What's a monthly?" I asked.

She told me. I kept shaking my head. It's hard to imagine that something pretty and soft is used for the Curse. "But what about womanhood rags?" I asked.

She scratched her head. "Womanhood rags?"

Know what, Clarissa?

The Woman said that I'm beginning to look as off as she thinks I am. That the way my shoulders hunch and my feet drag and the way I carry my head sideways makes me look like something awful is riding me and it needs to come out. She told me that my mind keeps wandering off to somewhere else, calls it being afflicted in a stupedor kind of way.

But I hunch my shoulders and hold my head sideways so that my plaits can touch my shoulders. Then I pretend they don't seem so short and dinky, and when someone calls me ugly I don't pay them any attention because I think they're talking to someone else.

My feet drag because that's what they want to do. So I drag them. And my mind wandering off—that's just what it does on its own too, I guess.

It's okay in a way. The Woman just laughs instead of getting mad like she did before. I wanted to cry when she first laughed but now I see that nothing else happens when she laughs and so her laughing is Glue.

"Ain't too much sense you can beat into a stupedor," the Woman said when she changed her mind about hitting me and laughed instead. "Just wear yourself out trying."

Sometimes I laugh with her when I know what she's laughing about. It's those things that seem to be right to me when I'm doing them but then seem wrong after they're done. Like the time when I cut the pee spot out of the sheet. I thought she wouldn't know if the spot wasn't there. When she found it she laughed and called me Stupedor.

Almost everyone's calling me Stupedor now. Sometimes the Woman calls me Odessa too. At times I call *myself* Stupedor, when I catch myself being stupid. But I hate being called Odessa. Odessa is Aunt Della's daughter who went crazy because she had the syphilis too long. I never had the syphilis but I did have an infection—down there. The Woman said that it came from filth and told me I had to use the basement toilet from then on until it went away, and to clean the toilet with bleach every time I used it. I couldn't wash in the bathroom either or eat near Marcus and James or touch anything.

She told Sister. Sister called me aside before recess and told me to use only one toilet in the restroom and to tell her which one it was so that she could make sure that nobody else used it. Some girls beat me up when they found out why I couldn't use the other toilets. Sister sent me home and the Woman told me that the girls wouldn't have beaten me up if I hadn't been filthy.

"When you *be* like filth," she said, "you gonna get *treated* like filth."

I'm still ashamed about it. Girls still stare at me when I go to the bathroom so I wait until everyone is out before I go in.

It hurts sometimes—being called afflicted. When people look at me and talk low so I can't hear them, and even worse when they talk to me like I might have a hard time understanding what they're saying to me. The most embarrassing though is when Sister pulls me aside to give me soap and sanitary napkins and then keeps me in at recess to tell me how to bathe myself and how to put the napkins on. It makes me feel like a pagan baby all over again.

Aunt Della told the Woman that she thinks my being afflicted might be a sign from God that she'd lived a life of ruination at some time and that He's making her pay for it. The Woman got so mad I thought she'd cut Aunt Della along with the chicken she was cutting up.

"That's a bald faced lie if I ever heard one," she said. "I always lived a clean life. It ain't got nothing to do with the way that child is!"

It didn't matter to Aunt Della that the Woman was mad. She said, "*Some*body's paying for something around here, I see, and that's all I got to say."

"If you do good, don't nothing but good follow," the Woman shot back. "God Himself knows I lived a good life."

Aunt Della didn't buy it. "You reap what you sow," she said. "So I know you did something you ain't told. Mine went off like that and you said yourself it was a sign from God I did something dissipating. Now it's your turn and you call it something else— Ellen, bring yourself over here!"

She took my shoulders and turned me around so the Woman could see me. "Look at this! Let me tell you, sister, you call it what it is. The apple ain't never fell too far from its tree, and if mine is caused by *me* lying in dirt, then you sure ain't no better.

"Who would've thought," Aunt Della went on almost to herself. "The Lord sure works His ways."

"Don't say nothing else, Della! I'm sick and tired of you bringing up the Lord and His ways. What in *hell* do you know about the Lord anyway, all the shit you did in your life? Odessa's paying today cause you couldn't keep your legs shut—

off from the syphilis cause of some no good man you picked up out there . . ."

Aunt Della took her bags and hurried up and got out before the Woman could say any more about Odessa.

The Woman thought about Aunt Della's words for about three or four days, then told the Root Worker she couldn't take it anymore.

"Haints just took over this here child," the Root Worker told her. "That's what's the matter with her. Not something you did. They get inside the ones that's off and weak. That's where they know they can make'm do anything—and they start to get queer-looking, like Ellen here. They act like it too cause they can't help it. Something else has a hold on the way they look and act."

She gave the Woman a little bottle with something orange-red in it and told her to put down a few drops of it in every room and to feed me, herself, from the same plate each time. "Don't wash it with the others," she told her. "Mix a drop of this stuff with alum and spread it over her plate, then put the plate in a brown paper bag up high on your backporch till it's time for her to eat again. You get what I'm telling you?"

The Woman nodded.

"Do that for eleven and a half days," the Root Worker said, "or until she have the Curse again, then burn the plate with the first rag. She might still look like that—can't change what's already done but what's in her won't get at you."

I imagined what a haint must look like—gnarled and witch-like and humped over from living a thousand years probably. With wild gray hair that looks like Brillo and eyes that are blood red and crazy. And I keep trying to look like one.

~

The Girlfriend died yesterday.

The Husband didn't cry, didn't even go to work. He didn't say anything when the Woman told him—just sat out in the garage and stared off at nothing all day. She didn't tell him in a loud voice like she did when she told him that she heard the Girlfriend went in for another operation. She almost whispered it, "Passed away, Della said—was six this morning," when he didn't ask her but moved his lips like he wanted to.

It was the way she said it—"passed away"—that made me think she would put her arms around the Husband and cry for him. He must have had the same thought. He stepped closer but she turned around suddenly and said, "Got clothes to wring."

That's all she did the rest of the day—wring. First the clothes, then the dishrag, then her hands, like she could wring the Girlfriend's death away.

"Heard it was the breast disease," Aunt Della said to the Woman's back. The Woman didn't answer, just dipped the mop in the bucket and wrung it out. "Heard it started in the pit, then spread to her breast—the left one," Aunt Della went on.

The Woman pushed the mop under the table, then dipped it in the bucket again. "Don't want to talk about it, Della."

"Missed the corner by the sink," Aunt Della said. Then ignoring what the Woman told her she said, "Wasn't down there, like it usually is. But the breast's a woman part just the same's the way I see it."

The Woman turned and screamed, "Shit, Della!"

Aunt Della backed away, then looked at the Woman like the disease was on her. "Aw, hell, you *laid* with him!"

"Della, you lost your mind?" the Woman asked.

Aunt Della stepped close to the Woman and took the mop. "It's cila work and you know it. Said so yourself—That's what cilas *do*, Della. Ain't my words, sister. Came straight out of your mouth, remember?" Her voice lowered. "Wouldn't be bothering you if you didn't lay with him."

"Wasn't the cila," the Woman whispered to the floor.

"What?"

"Killed her." She stopped and looked at me. "Ellen, come finish this floor."

I took the mop from Aunt Della.

"Dead, just as I'm breathing here," the Woman said to Aunt Della as they left the kitchen.

I followed them into the front room, then stopped when the Woman said, "Della, ain't a cila in the world worked that." She whispered, "Didn't nobody do that but me."

I remember the Girlfriend's drawers, Clarissa. I can still see them—big as Aunt Della's slips and brownish-pink. Remember the Root Worker taking them over to the window and holding them up to the light, squinting to read them. That's what she said she was doing, reading them—like they were the Sunday news. But I don't remember the odor they had.

That's what the Root Worker told the Woman she smelled on the drawers, the odor that was already there.

"Fixed or dead shouldn't be no mind to you," she laughed when the Woman told her that she couldn't sleep since the Girlfriend died.

The Woman stood up to leave. "Wasn't what I wanted. Killing just ain't me."

"What I meant was it shouldn't be no mind to you cause it wasn't what you did that killed her," the Root Worker hurried up and said. "Death was already on that woman when you came to me."

The Woman shook her head. "Easy to tell somebody . . ."

"Could smell it on the drawers."

The Woman scratched her head.

"You recall it," the Root Worker answered like she knew what the Woman might ask, "but it ain't came to you yet."

The Woman shut her eyes trying to remember. "She'd washed'm," she said when she could see the drawers again. "Had'm hanging on a line over her bathtub."

The Root Worker rubbed her neck. "Baby, that odor don't wash." She stood up and went over to the altar where she stared at the dead beautyshop lady's picture. "You recall, and I know you do. Might've hid it from your mind, and I don't blame you for it, but that odor comes back every time. Just like the spirits they belong to." She shut her eyes like the Woman. "Can smell it just as if it was here this minute, sweet and putrid. You know it. Like ain't cured yet meat that stayed out too long but still might have a little good left on it."

I smelled it myself when she talked about it but I still don't remember the odor. I don't think the Woman remembered either. She just took a deep breath and said, "All right, if you say it was."

The Root Worker stepped toward the Woman, then stopped and glanced over at me and smiled. "Well, recall or not," she said, "this child's what you need to keep your eye on cause it's no telling."

"Ellen?"

The Root Worker came around my chair and rubbed my shoulders. "They ride the weakest ones," she said.

The Girlfriend's funeral was at a little wooden church way out in the country. The Husband didn't go. The Woman told him it would be all right with her if he did but he said, "It's been enough."

I didn't think the Woman would go either but she told Aunt Della it was what she had to do. "There's something about the dead that'll keep wandering back if you don't see them off," she said.

It was a long ride to the church—some hundred fifty or so miles, the Woman said. Up near a place called Idlewild where rich colored people live in the summer. I didn't see Idlewild but I imagined it full of people in fur coats and long dresses, all with new Buicks like Reverend Blackwell's. I imagined him there telling the rich people they need to come back and worship at their roots.

"Don't see how she'd come to have a funeral way up there," the Woman said. "Except I heard mention they'd found a cousin who might be a dentist or something." That's who came to claim the body after a week or so. After nobody else would.

We drove for hours, Clarissa. The Woman stopped lots of times to ask the way. Most of the time people didn't answer her. They didn't even look at us, just kept walking, picking out tomatoes or talking to each other. The Woman didn't ask again, just took my arm and we slipped quietly back into the car. I thought we were invisible until she found a lady who told us to turn around, go a little further, then turn where the road forks.

We drove on and I dozed off until the Woman shook me awake. "Don't want you sitting up in church with sleep on your face," she said.

The houses and stores had disappeared. Gone except for a few houses hidden behind thick clumps of trees. The thick trees turned into big white houses with barns bigger than our house beside them. Into yards that led to treeless fields plowed into rows and rows of brown and green. The Woman said they were corn farms.

We found a store after we drove around lost for a while. An

old white man's. He nodded slowly when the Woman asked about the church. He scratched his chin. "Colored church? Know about where that might be," he said, then told her. She frowned. "Well, I'll just have to show you," he said.

We followed his pickup truck for about a half-hour, past barns and corn fields, through roads that stretched and twisted until the farms became smaller and the houses turned little and homemade like shacks that I had seen in my geography book. The old man blew his horn, then pointed at a big clump of trees ahead. "Up there," he hollered out the window. "About two miles in the thicket it'll be a clearing and you'll see it."

We got lost in the trees and the bumpy dirt road. The Woman almost gave up but she took another turn and we heard singing and shouting and tambourines down the road. We followed it straight to the tiny white painted church with PROGRESSIVE SPIRITUAL GUIDANCE SANCTIFIED handwritten on the door over a picture of Jesus painted brown.

The funeral wasn't at all quiet like Mr. Stevens's. The church rocked back and forth while people danced in the wood plank aisles. All over the church people stomped their feet and shook while they sang and clapped and hollered and cried all at the same time. The music got louder as they shook. I shook too and hoped that God wouldn't decide to strike the whole church with me in it. I made an Act of Contrition inside my head.

We started for a pew after the music stopped but a man in white gloves whispered something to the Woman. We followed him to the front of the church where the Girlfriend's casket sat in front of a light blue altar with a homemade cross. I stopped when I looked at the woman dressed in white inside the casket. She didn't look like the Girlfriend—didn't look real but like she was made out of polished wood. I reached over and touched her hand. It felt like wood too. *It's not her*, I thought. *Must be someone else.*

I turned around to follow the Woman back to our seats and stopped. There, sitting in the front pews, was a whole row of old women with Brillo-looking gray matted hair. Gnarled witch-looking women whose backs humped over from living a thousand years. Everything else stopped when I saw them—dancing stopped, music, everything.

The old women's eyes darted back and forth wildly in the quiet and looked straight through everything. One of them looked through me and she twitched. She kept looking. Then she laughed out loud and cried at the same time in words I didn't know.

*Haints.*

"It comes in threes," the Root Worker said. "Comes in threes and looks like what it ain't."

"Like Ellen?" the Woman asked.

The Root Worker shook her head. "Said it *rides* the child, not *is* her."

The Woman put her elbows on the table and cupped her head in her hands. "Can't figure out how come."

The Root Worker was quiet for a minute, then nodded her head. "Said she just up and left you didn't you?" She waited but the Woman didn't answer. "Cause she didn't want you here in the first place is how come!" She threw her hands up like the Woman should have figured it out herself. "Your own mama. Now it's you that's here and her that's gone—think she'd be satisfied with that?"

The Woman looked up at her.

"And she ain't gonna let you be at peace with it either. That's how come she works through this here child." She sat down across from the Woman and took both of her hands.

"Look, baby, ain't got a thing against that child—off ones can't help it. But I call what I see. I saw it when you walked in with her the day that woman died." She studied the Woman's face. "Figured that's how come you couldn't smell it—didn't even *smell* like itself." She stared at the Woman long and hard. "Death. Riding Ellen and chasing you."

The Woman looked at me and bit her lip. "Gonna kill me," she said to herself.

"Said it comes in threes," the Root Worker said. "First one could've been herself. Funny they never told you *how* she died, just that she did. Next it'll be somebody else . . ."

"What I put on that woman's what killed her," the Woman said.

The Root Worker squeezed her hand. "Ain't you—causing somebody to die. Know if you did it'd be on you from now on. So she took what you did—the fix—and made it do just that."

A sucking sound came from the Woman's throat.

"Wasn't nothing I could do," the Root Worker said. "It already was." She thought for a minute. "Third one's probably you. But it's something for that."

The Woman searched the Root Worker's eyes, then turned her head. "Next one'll be on me from now on too," she said.

"Bring me back sixty," the Root Worker said like she didn't hear the Woman. "Gotta send down to Robert Earl'nem."

The Woman doesn't say much to anyone, mostly talks to herself. "They do it in threes," she says like she's reminding herself. Sometimes she says, "Um, um, um! Poor woman left all those kids and no daddy," out loud. Other times she shuts herself up in the kitchen and just makes a sound that wails. Not crying but like the screams I hear from purgatory.

She didn't sleep last night, wouldn't let me sleep either. She woke me up and had me sit in a chair so she could watch me— said I might dream something bad up. That's what she says all the time now. Might do something. Says, "Don't touch that, Ellen—

might make somebody die," and "Don't go in there with Ellen, Marcus—might come down sick," or "Come in here where I can watch you, Ellen—might do something."

Everything's Death. That's the way she sees it. Tree limb broke, she said it's a sign of Death. An old woman smiled at her, she said, "Must be Death." And I can't let her hear me talk to you, says I'm seeing Death and it's talking to me. That's when she takes the Root Worker's stuff. I don't know what it is but she takes it a lot and she keeps going back for more.

Marcus makes a game out of it when we're outside. Says, "Can't put Death on me, Ellen," then runs and hollers "Glue!" when I almost catch him.

James is scared I know. He didn't say he is, doesn't say anything. Just cuts his eyes at me every now and then. I don't know, makes me laugh sometimes. The Woman says that's Death laughing and James gets quiet all of a sudden.

~

"They say I got a baby, Ellen," James said.

*Who you gonna tell, Ellen?* I shook my head. "Flushed it."

He opened his mouth, then slumped his shoulders and put his head in his hand. "Ellen, that time . . ." The rest stuck inside his throat.

I didn't know what else to say to him so I said the first thing I could think of. "They took it?"

He shook his head. "Saw it yesterday. A girl. Don't look much like me . . ." I didn't hear the rest, he said it too low.

I tried to see the baby inside my head. All I could see was its eyes looking like the baby's eyes that I used to see. So I thought about the Woman and the Husband and then I could see its whole face. It looked like me.

"Getting married?" I asked.

He laughed. "Ain't even turned nineteen yet, Ellen."

He looks a lot older. Most women think he's older too, he says—at least twenty-five. And they all think he looks good. Marcus doesn't pay him much mind, says he brags too much about his looks. He is good looking, Clarissa, but I don't think about it when he talks to me. Or think about how old he looks. I don't say much most of the time, just listen. He talks mostly when I sit out on the steps when it's too late for people to be out. I know he doesn't want anyone to see him talking to me but I want him to sit out with me just the same. So I try to sit out late as much as I can.

He didn't say much the first few times, just sat on the step like it might be a good thing for him to do. Sometimes he'd say, "Ellen, that time . . ." or "You know I didn't mean to . . ." But it stuck in his throat like it just did when I said "flushed it." Then he'd get quiet and we would just sit for a while until he laughed and said, "Getting kind of late, ain't it?"

One night I said, "Some girls said you're cute, James," when it stuck, because I knew it would be something he'd like to hear.

He grinned and said, "You know I had one almost thirty."

*Who had you, Ellen?*

I think James must have heard my thought because he hurried up and said, "Didn't go all the way like . . ." and stuck again.

"What's Death look like?" he asked me the first time he came out to the steps. He didn't sit then, just stood on the top step behind me and said it to my back. Real low so that nobody else could hear him.

"What's Death look like, Ellen?"

I stiffened. "Huh?"

"Death," he said. "Aunt Della said she heard you can see it."

I didn't say anything.

"Just want to know what it looks like, Ellen." He choked the words.

I turned around. He held his hands up. "Won't mess with you, Ellen, I swear."

I stared out at the streetlight and tried to imagine what Death might look like. I saw the combs with the thread knotted around them.

James stepped down closer and stopped. "Huh, Ellen?"

*Saw it when you walked in with her the day that woman died*, the Root Worker said.

"Almost blue," I whispered.

"Blue?"

"Like the Girlfriend," I said. "So black it's almost blue."

The bread fell off the shelf again.

No matter how many loaves it is that I put on the pantry shelf one of them will always fall.

The Woman saw the loaf fall this morning and told me to put it back on the shelf. I picked it up off the floor and put it back on the shelf. She watched for a while and it didn't fall.

Later we were in the front room cutting up rags and I heard the bread fall. I kept cutting. The Woman stopped and looked over at me for a long time then told me to come with her to the pantry.

A loaf of bread was on the floor.

"Third one," she whispered.

"That's what they *do*, baby. Bring it right back to you the way you give it," the Root Worker said.

The Woman sucked in her breath and stared right through me. I looked at my shoelaces.

"Know it's the sign," the Root Worker went on. "It's the same way you took it to her—in the bread you took her kids." She scratched her chin. "You said yourself Ellen's the one took the bread in her door. Now Ellen's the one put it up and it falls. That tell you something?"

The Woman was quiet for a minute then said, "Ought to put her out."

"Can't *put* it out, you got to *wait* it out," the Root Worker said. "Told you that, said you got to wait for it and then you can look it dead in the eye and be glad it's over cause the third's the last."

"Won't be glad if it's me," the Woman said.

The Root Worker took her hand. "Don't know who but I can tell you this much, ain't gonna be you cause I gave you something."

The boys are singing on the corner again.

I heard them last night too, singing to the beat that their fingers snapped. *Ooh-ooh, baby, ba-bayh—doo wop wop wop ooh.*

When I close my eyes I can see them in my head looking just like James, with slicked-back hair that's as shiny and black as patent leather. The Woman said that's what brought him Death— seeing him in my head.

"It was a cat," I said. But she didn't listen, just wrung her hands and cried, "Why didn't you see me instead?"

But I didn't see the cat either. Not until Madeline said, "That the cat you talked to in the bushes, Ellen?" just as James stepped out on the porch.

I turned around and saw it. Pretty and black as blue. The Woman said that's why James knew it was the Girlfriend, Clarissa. It was blue-black like her. He saw it and hollered, "Get her away from me, Ellen," before I knew what "her" was.

"What—" I turned to ask him, then stopped right in the middle.

Sweat beads had popped out all over his forehead and he had turned as dark as the night, then gray.

All of a sudden he jumped over the two bottom steps and ran out in the street right into a car. It hit him, threw him into the air. He bounced off the hood just like he was nothing and landed flat on his back near the car's front wheels. And it rolled right over his head and kept going.

James twitched on the ground under the streetlight like his insides were all fighting to get out.

I sat still on the step, thought it wouldn't be real if I didn't move. Almost at the same time I thought it I found myself out in the street next to where he lay. Something lay on top of his head and it breathed in and out like trying to catch its breath. It reminded me of the thing that came out of me, only it was sort of yellowish.

I screamed and nothing came out of my mouth.

The Woman showed up from nowhere and fell on her knees in the middle of the black street. "Killed him!" she cried. And then she pressed her whole body down on the street. A moan came out of her, then words. "Don't do this. Don't *do* it. Don't do it, *Ellen!* Knew it'd be something . . . Lord, not this!"

I saw the Cila Lady's combs with the knots that I had tied around them still under my blanket. Still there.

The Woman lifted her head. Her face wasn't pretty anymore, just long with twists and knots. She squeezed her eyes tight and it pulled her mouth and opened the side of it. I thought it would be a scream but it was a siren that came out of it, Clarissa. It came out low—long and slow. It grew and shrieked loud and high, shattering the Cila Lady's combs.

Someone pushed me and the people crowded around me. They cried and screamed and cursed. The Husband came out, put his arm around me, and pulled me toward the porch. At first it felt good around me, safe. But then I thought it might make something happen to him too, so I shrugged his arm away and ran to the porch. The old man next door went inside his house and came back out with root powder that he poured all around his porch. He made the Sign of the Cross, and said, "Damn! Damn!"

That's all he said. "Damn!"

~

Last week when the Woman was out Aunt Della came over and went upstairs to change into her church clothes. She came back downstairs and asked whose bed was that in the little corner room off from the attic. I told her it was mine. She asked me if I felt bugs crawling on me and biting me when I slept in it. I said that I hadn't. She pulled me into the dining room and made me take my blouse off so that she could see my back and arms.

"All those bites on you and you don't feel nothing?" she asked.

I had those little red marks for as long as I can remember but they never hurt or anything.

"No," I said. "Guess I'm just used to them."

"*Used* to'm!" she hollered. "How in hell can somebody be *used* to something crawling all over'm and biting the hell out of'm?" She handed me my blouse. "It's a shame before God—put it back on. Somebody ought to call the board of health. She'd have done it in a minute if it was one of mine, and wouldn't have been stutting what I thought about it."

The Woman took the board of health lady upstairs to look at my bed first and then at Marcus's bed. The lady told the Woman that Marcus's bed was okay but she had to get rid of my mattress because it was crawling with chinch bugs. As soon as the lady left the Woman called Aunt Della and told her she was no kind of a kin to her and cursed her to everything she could think of.

"You should've died instead of your boyfriend!" she said and slammed the phone down.

Aunt Della came over anyway a little while later and they

cussed and screamed at each other some more. Then Aunt Della began to talk to the Woman just like she hadn't just finished screaming at her. She told her that we should burn the mattress instead of leaving it out in the alley for the junk man. If we just left it out there, she said, the bugs would crawl back into the house.

The Woman scratched her head. "What I don't know is what she's gonna sleep on now," she said to Aunt Della. "Can't buy her another one—money's short."

"The floor," Aunt Della laughed like the Woman should have easily thought about it herself.

The Woman looked at her like she was out of her mind. "Can't no child of mine sleep on the floor," she said. "It'd be a disgrace."

"It'll be a bigger disgrace to ruin another good mattress like that," Aunt Della said. "You need to let her just sleep on the floor like she should've been sleeping on all along. Only make her put down some plastic to keep from ruining the floor too. And make her scrub it up to keep from getting all those chinch bugs again."

"And beat her ass," she added. "You got to beat her ass *before* she goes to sleep—that way she'll have something to think about all night and she'll get her lazy self up."

The Woman burned my mattress.

I dragged it to the alley and she set it on fire. I watched it burn. I watched the flames dance like little fire people around the cloth part first. Then they skipped over to melt the buttons and the thread that held them in place. I heard the fire people sing in my head and watched them dance and twist little flame knots—yellow, red, and blue. I moved closer and watched the little chinch bugs run all over the mattress trying to find Glue before the fire people could catch them.

I thought about the candles and the Bibles again and I could smell the ammonia pee smell that wakes me up every day, that stays caught between my nose and throat where I can almost taste it too. I felt it burn my eyes and sting my sores. I felt when the Woman whipped you, Clarissa—"Too lazy to get up!" she'd scream—every day almost, until she felt sorry enough for me and tired enough to give up and stop.

"Just can't do it anymore," she said.

I thought about kids laughing when I dragged that mattress out on the porch—a thousand times—for all of them to see what I had done. And after a thousand times they still laughed.

I watched it burn and it seemed all right.

~

Barbara might do my hair.

That's what the Cila Lady's real name is. Barbara. I found out today.

She told me that I can call her Barbara too. Not Miss So-And-So or *Miss* Barbara or anything—just Barbara.

The Woman met her when we took stuff out to the alley to sell to the junk man. The Woman told Marcus and me to stay out there with her in case he tried to cheat her. She wasn't in an arguing mood she told us, and if he tried we would haul the stuff right back in till he could come back with some sense.

The Woman waited while Barbara argued with the junk man about how much her old piano weighed. She told him that she knew it was heavier than he said it was because the men weighed everything on the truck and charged her by the weight of every single thing when they moved her from Saint Louis.

"That's right," the Woman called over to Barbara. "Been knowing that old fool for the longest. He'd cheat his own mama if he thought he'd make a nickel."

We weren't supposed to bother the junk man's horse. The

Woman said it's old and carries diseases and he has no business with a horse in the city and the people ought to do something about it. But we pulled grass up from inside the yard and tried to make the horse eat it anyway while the Woman and Barbara argued with the junk man. The horse didn't pay us any attention—looked like his mind was on a farm somewhere away from all the arguing and all the work.

The junk man must have given them what they wanted. He loaded all of the stuff onto his wagon and rode away.

Barbara stayed and talked with the Woman for a long time, then told her that she did hair on the side and said she wanted to do mine. She waved me over and I acted like I didn't see her. But the Woman did and she hollered, "Don't you see a grownup telling you to come here?" I went over to where they stood.

Barbara pulled me closer and studied my hair the way she had studied the weeds when we talked at the fence. She told the Woman that as coarse as my hair is it should take a press and curl okay. The Woman said that she didn't have any money and she'd just be wasting her time. But Barbara said she would do it for nothing just to see how it would look.

"Shirley's too old to be wearing plaits anyway," Barbara said while she looked in my hair and felt around the scalp. "About time she got used to having some kind of style to it."

"Shirley?" the Woman squinted at me. "Ellen, you been—"

"I thought I heard that boy over there call her Shirley," Barbara cut in quick. "Must have heard him wrong."

"Won't make her *look* no better," the Woman said. "Getting her hair done and all. She don't care none about what she looks like. Just lives with what God put on her. Ain't that right, Ellen?"

I didn't say anything, just looked down at Barbara's red toenails.

"You could use a good do too," Barbara said to the Woman. "Got good face bones, could bring it out."

"Well—" the Woman started.

"See, Ellen's is coarse." She fingered one of my plaits. "It'll stand more heat than yours. If I practice on hers a few times yours won't use much heat."

The Woman thought for a minute then told Barbara she'd think about it.

Then Barbara talked about the junk man. I stared at her toe-nails until she left.

Barbara came with her straightening combs and curlers and the Woman told her no. Aunt Della raised her eyebrow and looked at her but didn't say anything to her or Barbara. When Barbara left, the Woman told Aunt Della it was the wrong time of the month and she wasn't going to wash her hair or let anyone touch hers or mine. Aunt Della looked like she knew something then and said, "Well, can't fault you for that."

Barbara came again this afternoon in her little car. I guess she was on her way back from the church on Chene Street. The Woman met her at the door and said she'd send me right then.

Barbara said, "I have to make a stop first, so I guess I should take her and bring her back tonight."

We rode forever, Clarissa. And Barbara talked forever too. But I didn't listen, just pressed my nose to the window and tried to figure out how she could scrunch herself into the little car all the time, and why her head didn't touch the roof. Mine almost touched it and she's a lot taller. Her words meshed together in sounds and whispers that melted into the blurred houses and buildings that passed by the car window. And I kept my nose to the window still wondering until the houses and beautyshops became trees.

I sat up in the seat and stopped wondering, just looked at

clean brick houses with a lot of grass in front. They turned into fancy stores with dressed-up windows and white fancy signs. Not LIQUOR, not CANDLES AND INCENSE written on them. Not many people either—just clean and new stores.

We stopped in front of one that said FRIEBAUGH'S. "Well, we're here," Barbara said and got out. I didn't know where here was. I just sat and looked out at the store. She opened my door and said, "Ellen, I didn't bring you to sit in the car."

I followed her inside the big white doors with a lot of little windows. It was big and white inside too. Everything—counters, even the floors—white. It smelled good like perfume. I looked around at statues of white ladies who wore real dresses and shoes all fancy. I thought they were real at first but they didn't budge, just kept smiling. And they all looked up at the ceiling with one hand raised like they were amazed at what was up there. I looked up too and the ceiling was full of little lights—and white.

A lady who looked just like she was one of the statues sat a bag like the one that Barbara's combs were in on the counter. Barbara paid her and the lady handed her the bag.

She smiled like the statues and said, "Come back to see us."

Barbara's house isn't like everyone else's. It looks the same on the outside, kind of dusty and dark and ugly. But everything inside looks new and beige and green. And it smells like the store she took me to.

Barbara called me into the kitchen that was the same size as ours. Everything in it was in the same place too—cabinets, table, window, pantry. But everything in it was new. Clean and beige and new.

She gave me a peanut butter sandwich on a glass leaf-shaped plate and some milk in a glass cup that matched the plate. And a napkin. I didn't know how to eat the sandwich, Clarissa. It seemed like there must have been a special way to eat in a house like hers and I didn't know what that way was. So I nibbled around the sandwich and left the milk alone. I folded the napkin on the table, then unfolded it and wrapped the bottom of the sandwich in it, then nibbled around it some more. Barbara sat across from me and smiled the whole time. It made me feel like I should hurry up, so I did.

She cleared the table and said, "Let's do that head now."

It didn't hurt when Barbara washed and pressed my hair. I was so scared though, I couldn't hold still. She said she could tell I wasn't used to sitting still because I have so many scabs in my head. She asked why I was scared and quiet. I told her I might say something that would make her mad when the hot straightening comb was near my head. She said that's okay she'll talk for me. So she talked to me while she pulled the straightening comb through my hair. And she answered for me every time she asked me something.

She said funny things too and laughed out loud at what she had said. I kept my mouth shut and wiggled around in her beautyshop chair until I couldn't help it and laughed too. She didn't get mad, just laughed some more, and I imagined it must be the way God makes people laugh up in heaven. Then I imagined that it *was* heaven, I just didn't see God. I imagined that Barbara was the Woman and that she liked me because we had made it there.

She said, "Hold still so I can get the hair near your neck," and I stopped imagining.

She didn't burn me one time.

Barbara told the Woman that she should send me over every week because when I sweat the hair press goes back home. I didn't know what she meant and I didn't ask her.

She didn't say much when she pressed it this time, just "Hold your head this way," "Hold real still now," and "Move a little over that way."

She stopped and pulled a stool over, sat on it, and turned my chair around to face hers. She didn't say anything, just looked at me like she was waiting for me to say something.

I tried to laugh like we had done the last time but she looked serious so I stopped.

"What happened to your baby?" she finally asked.

"Nothing," I said.

"Then you still have it?"

"Flushed it."

A low *whoob* sucked from her mouth and caught in the air before it was all the way out.

"What did it feel like?" she asked.

"Didn't feel it."

"To flush your baby I meant?"

I looked through her glasses to find her eyes. I wanted to see them, don't know why, just did. They looked back at me like they were yours looking back from the windows and mirrors. I thought they were until I saw the little spider lines that fanned from their corners. And the scar was missing. Someone else's eyes, Clarissa. I never got that close to any. But I fixed my eyes on hers anyway. And I saw myself inside them.

"Like shit," I said to her eyes.

"Shit?"

"Yes, ma'am. Felt like I flushed shit."

She looked away. "Can't see doing something like that," she said. "But if it was by your own father . . . guess that can change the way you see a lot."

"Wasn't the Husband's," I whispered.

She turned back around.

"You mean he's not your real father?"

"He's my real daddy but it wasn't his."

"But they *think* it was," she said like she had to explain it to me. "Ellen, you should have told them whose it was."

I looked at the floor.

She searched for my eyes this time. "Why didn't you tell them?"

"Didn't know whose it was," I said.

The *whooh* stuck in the air again. She broke it. "But your father must have done *something* to you. You don't like him too much."

"He didn't do anything," I said. "I do. I like him a lot."

"People don't just go around calling their fathers the *Husband*, Ellen." Her voice shook. "It's Father or Daddy or something— not the *Husband* like they're not even related." She shook her head. "And you live under the same roof," she said. "Mine desert- ed me and I still call him Father."

She pulled my chair around and went back to straightening my hair. She didn't say anything else except, "Hold still while I get this side."

*We can't call him that*, I said over and over in my head until it sounded right. I pushed it out when she laid the straightening comb down.

"We can't call him that. Any of it. Not Father or Papa or Daddy. The Woman said none of us can. Could. James is dead. It'd remind her that she laid with him and it makes her sick, so we just call him the Husband." I couldn't stop to breathe or the rest would have slipped back down into my throat.

"The Woman . . . your real mother?"

"Yes, ma'am."

"And you have to call her the Woman," she said almost to herself.

"Just me, not Marcus."

"Let me get this side," she said and pulled the straightening comb through my hair.

After we had been quiet for a long time, she said, "Mine was a girl. Andrea Elizabeth. I remember what she felt like, what she smelled like. Funny, I even remember what she had on the day they came and took her. But I don't remember what she looked like." She laughed. "Don't remember what *he* looked like either, anything about him except that his name was Junior, he was about twenty, and I was in love. Junior who? I don't even know. Just that his name was Junior and I told him that I loved him.

"He never said he loved me, just If you love me prove it, when I told him. And I did every time I love you Junior came out of my mouth. But he never said it back, just demanded proof and took it."

I saw James and Leslie Stevens when she told me that, Clarissa.

"He moved away when I told him I was pregnant," she said. "Never saw him again. I was going on sixteen—a little older than you are. I hid it from Uncle Claude as long as I could, scared he'd put me out. He was all that I had. But he didn't put me out. He was disappointed at first. Worried a lot too."

She turned my chair around. "When I was about seven months or so, he told me that he had found someone who wanted my baby. It didn't bother me when he told me. In a way I was glad it would be over. But when I had her and named her, then held and nursed her for six weeks it all changed. When they came I begged and screamed and they couldn't pry her from my arms. They thought I might squeeze her to death, so they sat and waited like vultures waiting to pick a carcass. Uncle Claude told me that I wouldn't have a future with a baby at sixteen. I said, So what? Then he told me that the baby wouldn't have a future either. I smelled her one last time, fixed her little plait, and gave her to them."

She combed my hair to one side, turned my chair and studied my face, then pulled her iron curlers from the table drawer and laid them on the hot plate. She didn't say anything, just waited. I watched the tips turned red, then the smoke that curled out of them in a long stream and disappeared before it touched the ceiling.

She pulled the curlers off the burner and spit on them and the spit sizzled and disappeared as quickly as it landed. She rubbed the curlers across a towel and they left black streaks at first, then brown ones, then nothing. She lifted a piece of my hair and I heard the curlers click. "Think I'll try some crokonos this time," was all she said.

When I thought it might be all right to talk again I asked, "Where's your baby now?"

"Andrea? Oh she's a big girl now—going on thirteen. Only three years from where I was when she was conceived—probably filled out and everything. Hope there's no Juniors where she lives," she laughed.

"She's here somewhere, I believe. Uncle Claude said the people he gave her to were from Detroit. We tried to find them before he died but they had moved. So I wonder a lot. Even wondered if you might have been her, looking like you didn't quite fit, Uncle Claude's ways . . . I don't know. Makes you try to make every coincidence point to the improbable. Around the corner from where my father lived . . . maybe he sent those people to take her. Maybe he wanted her near because he missed me. Those thoughts went through my head more than a few times."

I tried to say, "I feel like I must be her too," but something lumped up in my chest and moved up to my throat. So I just thought it, thought, *I'm really her only my name is just the Elizabeth part of what you named her*, because I like Elizabeth best.

Barbara turned the chair around to face the mirror. "What do you think?" she asked.

I thought my hair looked pretty. And I thought I looked sort of funny and kind of pretty at the same time and that my face didn't seem to look quite as big anymore. But I just smiled and said, "Okay."

That's when she noticed the tooth that's not there anymore. "What happened to that tooth?" she asked and I shut my mouth.

"Shouldn't hide it, just a character mark like this." She took her glasses off and pointed to a little dark bean-looking knot at the top of her cheek that her glasses had hid. "A keloid," she said. "Got it when I was eight—fell off a bike." She put her glasses back on and the knot was hidden again. "Just sets my face off from everyone else's—gives it character like yours. How'd you lose your tooth?"

"Fell in some bushes," I said.

She raised an eyebrow. "Be right back," she said, then went upstairs.

She came back with a scarf and tied it around my head. "So it won't sweat and nap up," she said. "Tie it like this when you go to bed."

"Want you to have this too," she said. And she gave me a bottle of Evening in Paris that was just like the Woman's only smaller. "You'll soon be a woman," she said when she gave me the perfume. "You have to get used to looking and smelling like one."

I put them under my blanket with the combs.

Everyone at school's been telling me that my hair looks nice, including Sister and the Little Monkeyshine Boy. He said that I look kind of cute now with my hair fixed like this. I think he likes me.

Barbara pressed my hair again because it sweated and napped up. The Woman told her that my hair would come out if she pressed and curled it too much. But Barbara said that it had already been coming out before she did it so it wouldn't make any difference. The Woman still wasn't going to let her do it again but Aunt Della told her that she should let anyone do it who's crazy enough to put up with me and that I might stop peeing in the bed if I got used to looking like something.

I still pee in the bed—not really in the bed but on the plastic on the floor. I stopped for a few days and thought I had stopped for good. But one morning I woke up and two of Aunt Della's boys who had spent the night were standing over me. One of them said, "Watch this, Ellen."

He pulled his thing out of his drawers and peed all over me and the plastic. Some of it got in my hair and they laughed. All I could do was just lay there and pee on myself too.

Barbara gave me a new dress. She said that it used to be hers and that she had been saving it for Andrea but it would be just as good if I had it. It's a pretty light green one with little puffed-up pink butterflies all over. All I can do most of the time now is think about it. Never have I ever seen anything so pretty, Clarissa.

The Woman told Barbara to take the dress back because it was too good for me to mess up but Barbara told her that it used to be hers and seeing me in it would be a big favor to her. She didn't mention that she had given me the scarf and perfume or the combs. I won't wear them—the Woman might get mad. But I'll wear the dress. I stayed awake so I could get up in the middle of the night to try it on. It makes me look pretty I thought when I looked at myself in it. I thought about the Little Monkeyshine Boy. How he won't even believe that it's really me when he sees me. He'll ask Marcus who I am because he'll never have seen any-one in his life who's as beautiful. And I was glad that his name wasn't Junior. I thought about it all night.

I thought about the Woman too. That she'll just look at me and be glad.

"Thank God!" she'll say. And that would be enough.

I looked in the mirror a hundred times.

I combed my hair a hundred times too until it looked just right.

I went downstairs before the Woman got up and made a pot of coffee. I heard her coming and poured a cup and waited. She came into the kitchen and I handed the cup to her and smiled. I said good morning in the best voice that I could. She said, "Morning, Ellen," but nothing else. I was still smiling when she finished the coffee and put the cup in the sink. I trembled.

She started to reach under the cabinet for the skillet. I ran over and got it for her, then stood and waited still smiling. Still nothing else. She headed toward the pantry and bumped into me.

"Ellen," she said. "If you don't get yourself in there and sit down somewhere . . ."

I went into the front room, put my coat on, and waited for Marcus.

After about a half-hour had passed the Woman came in and told me to take the coat off, it would be a while before Marcus would even wake up. I took it off. She just stood there for a moment and didn't say a word. And then she laughed.

"Lord, if that don't beat all," she said. "That dress of hers just fits, Ellen. Brings some life into you and everything." She went back into the kitchen laughing.

I laughed and then I smiled again.

That was good enough.

# LOVE AND
# RUINED FRUIT

Barbara's house is the only white one.

It seems like it should be invisible in the snow. But it's the only one around here that you can see most of the time. The rest have old brown and yellowed paint that fades into nothing.

They remind me of the Root Worker's woodcrate altar that would be invisible without the candles. Ours is fading too.

Reverend and his twin brother painted Barbara's last October. Now it shines. Her windows shine too and the snow sends jewels off them sometimes blue, sometimes green, sometimes both. It hurts your eyes to look at them when the sun's real bright.

Reverend asked Barbara to marry him. The print's still in the snow where he got down on his knees all of a sudden and said, "Ellen is my witness here, I'm asking you to marry me."

That's what Barbara calls her boyfriend. Reverend. His real name is Waymon Toulis but the people at her church call him *Reverend* Toulis because he's like their priest, she said. She just calls him Reverend.

I asked her why they didn't call him Father like we call Father Ritkowski and she smiled and said I ask a lot of questions now since I've decided to open up and talk to her more. She never did say why they didn't call him Father so I just call him Reverend too. It's fine with him, he says, because he's been calling me Elizabeth since Barbara told him that's what I want my name to be.

I don't know how I feel about her marrying him. She asked me, "What do you think, Ellen?" when he was still on his knees and I said, "It's all right I guess."

I like him but I think about him laying with her and getting her pregnant.

I do ask her a lot of questions. Not about God and sin anymore. Mostly ones like why do I bleed if it's not a curse. She told me but I still don't understand. She still doesn't understand why I call the Woman the Woman either.

What's the biggest puzzle, she said, is you Clarissa. She said that last week then turned around and said, "Clarissa is really you isn't she, Ellen?"

I said no and she shook her head and left it at that.

The Woman has a boyfriend. His name is Mr. Harper and he comes over when the Husband's at work. He's not handsome, he's kind of wiry and old-looking with frog eyes. And he has hair missing from the top of his head. He smells like mint and wipes his shoes off all the time too. He holds his hat in his hands and talks proper, calls the Woman my sweet love. He says, "How are you, my sweet love?" and "My but don't you look just lovely today," to the Woman, then "How do, young sir," to Marcus. The Woman says he courts, that's what she likes about him. She doesn't get sick anymore. She said he makes her feel like a new woman and she doesn't care who the Husband has.

He didn't try to kiss her when he first started coming over. He used to say, "I'm here to talk business with the lady," when I let him in. Then one day the Woman said, "You don't have to pay Ellen much mind, she's slow."

Now he doesn't say anything to me just "Here, hang my coat up and don't wrinkle it," and then goes straight to the kitchen to put his arms around the Woman.

I slipped on one of Marcus's shoes last week when I went to hang the coat. My head hit the side of the door and blood got on the sleeve. The Woman hollered, "Ellen, shit!" then said, "Excuse me, I forgot myself" to Mr. Harper.

Mr. Harper's smile left and something that looked like evil came into his eyes. It left as soon as it came and his smile was back. He patted the Woman's arm and said, "I can't believe those lips could say such words." Then he said, "Young lady, go get some cold water and rub it easy and make sure you don't mess it up."

They went back to smiling and hugging until it was time for him to leave and I gave him his coat. He looked at me like he was worried and said, "Looks like it might be quite nasty that cut on your head. You need to put cold water on it," just like he said about his coat sleeve.

It stopped bleeding by itself.

One time Mr. Harper said, "Let's go upstairs and get some privacy," to the Woman.

She said, "I'm not that type, Mr. Harper."

He slapped his forehead and said, "What can I be saying? Forgive me for losing myself, it's just that you're so beautiful."

Marcus thinks he's funny.

The Woman is pretty again. Not beautiful like she was when her hair was long, just pretty in a way that's cute. Barbara comes over and does her hair every Saturday and she cuts it sometimes. The Woman tells her to do it before it gets long again. She said it's better short because it makes her face look not as long. I liked it better long but I tell her she's prettier that way when she asks me.

The Woman smiles all the time when Mr. Harper's here. In-love smiles. She talks proper too, says darling and dear the way the ladies do when they're in love on television. Even to me says "Ellen, dear" this and "Ellen, be a darling and get me such and such."

Most days I cut through the alley to Barbara's after I hang up Mr. Harper's coat. The Woman said I shouldn't spend so much time over there since Barbara has a boyfriend. But I think she said it just for Mr. Harper to hear because when it looks like I might stay sometimes she'll say, "Go ask that lady when can she do our hair again."

I ask then stay until it's time for the Husband to come home.

I don't see much of the Root Worker anymore—only twice since Mr. Harper. Both times the Woman said she needed something to keep Mr. Harper's shoes at her door. The Root Worker gave her something different each time and she rushed back to put it on the porch before Mr. Harper got here. The second time must have worked because it was the last time I saw the Root Worker except once at the store. That's when she told me to go home and ask the Woman if she had aches in the area of her womb.

I didn't ask her.

I don't see Aunt Della anymore either. Not since Mr. Harper told the Woman she should think again about letting her come over so much. "I know how sisters get and it makes relations bad," he said. Then he said, "Tell her easy."

Aunt Della swole up bigger than herself when the Woman told her and said, "He's the one that's wrong for being here, you still a married woman. And it makes you the same as your man."

The Woman said something I didn't hear and Aunt Della said, "Well I don't take kinship with him or nothing he has to say and I'll tell him myself!"

Aunt Della told him the next time he came over. The Woman stayed in the kitchen while she did. Aunt Della told him loud with plenty of words and ended it with, "And I'll kick your ass and have you wipe it up!"

Mr. Harper didn't talk back, just sat with his legs crossed and listened, then called the Woman from the kitchen.

"Sweet love, come over here," he said. The Woman wiped her hands on her dress and came over to where he sat. He stood up and walked around her. Aunt Della swole up again and screamed, "You heard me!" He still didn't say anything to her. Just put his hands on the Woman's waist and leaned over until his nose touched her hair.

"Rose Hips," he said and the Woman looked back at him and smiled.

"Me or her," he said into her hair. "She's yours and you love her for it, I know. And I love her for it too. But you have to decide."

That was the last time I saw Aunt Della for a while.

Mr. Harper told the Woman the same thing about the Husband too—You have to decide—just a little over a month after he started coming over.

"Can't just put him out of his own house," the Woman told him. "He don't bother me—don't even ask to lay with me. And he puts food on the table, I can say that for him."

"It's him or me," he said just like he did with Aunt Della.

"Mr. Harper, I got to have sense and look at it this way," she said. "We've been together going on twenty years and he always took care of me. We had our times but we go our own ways now and it's fine. You don't put a dog out in the street if it ain't bothering nobody."

"Him or me," he repeated like she hadn't said anything.

"You gonna take care of all us?" she asked.

Mr. Harper slapped himself and said, "How could I have been

so inconsiderate? It's just that I can't bear these moments without you."

The Husband studies the Bible with a new lady who knocks on people's doors and asks them to let her teach them about what God wants. She calls it working in the field. The Husband said he thinks he'll work in the field too as soon as he learns enough about the Bible. I waited for the Woman to explode when he told her that but she just looked like she didn't believe him, then said, "If it makes you happy."

He hasn't been studying long, just two or three weeks. Last month he went to all of the Help Keep Saint Agnes Open meetings. Father Ritkowski came by and told him and the Woman that everyone should help because Saint Agnes might close since most of the white people have left the parish.

"We weren't really part of Saint Agnes in the first place," the Woman said to him.

Father Ritkowski turned red and didn't say anything else but the Husband said, "I'll be there for both of us."

The Husband went to the meetings every time they called him and brought home new stuff about Saint Agnes to give to people. Then the fieldwork lady started coming by. He told Father Ritkowski he wasn't feeling well one time, then he just couldn't make it the next, until he just didn't go to the meetings anymore.

Sister said we shouldn't worry, they'll probably stay open two or three more years and then they'll find another school for us. But I don't want to leave Saint Agnes, especially since Madeline's there now and she's my best friend next to Marcus. And I'll miss Sister. She smiles different now. She calls me over sometimes when I pass her talking to another Sister in the hall and says, "I like this new Ellen." She said that Madeline's making me talk more. It's really because of Barbara and Reverend but I won't tell her, she might say I shouldn't be with them so much since they're not Catholic.

Marcus says it's because I'm getting independent. He said he knows because I don't act like I need to catch up with him all the time anymore. "But I want you to walk with me now," he said. "You look nice sometimes."

I think he wants to walk with me because he wants to be near Madeline, he's still in love. He acts silly when he's near her and we both pretend that we don't see him.

~

Saint Agnes is closing in June.

So is the new school that they were going to send us to and two others. Sister said they're going to put most of the kids together in a bigger school somewhere near Grosse Pointe. She called it consolidating.

But we won't be going, found that out this morning. Sister said the fund that's sponsored us all this time is closing too. The Woman said that's because the rest of the white people don't plan on staying in Detroit much longer. Sister said the Archdiocese will keep the church open and just close the school. And we have to keep going to Mass just the same and to Confession.

"I don't know where you're going to go yet," she said. "But I want you to take what you learned in religion wherever you go."

I can't think of much that I learned in religion anymore, Clarissa. Except some things about God, hell, martyrs, and Confession. That mixes in with what I learned from Barbara and Reverend and it all mixes with what I think I know from the Root Worker's. So I try not to think of any of it, that's why I don't ask questions about God anymore.

The Root Worker is moving too. She'll be opening an emporium.

It's a big store where she can reach more people because she'll have more in it, she told the Woman. It's the good-looking building two doors down from Reverend's church she said. She'll open it next month if she can do something about Reverend and his people.

"What do they have to do with it?" the Woman asked.

"They've been going door to door telling folks God and what I do don't mix," the Root Worker said. "I tell'm that's where I got it from. God. Heard he's going downtown on me sometime soon but ain't a law down there says I can't open. He knows it so he's calling all the people to meet."

"You worried?" the Woman asked.

"Can't say I ain't," the Root Worker told her.

"He said, physician, heal thyself," the Woman mumbled.

The Root Worker scratched her head. "What?"

"Then use your stuff," the Woman said.

~

I'll be in Barbara's wedding in two days.

They want to get married before she gets too much along or she'll be too big to fit in her dress.

"That's what they said about me," I said. "Before it gets too much along."

"I'm sorry," she whispered.

"It's okay," I said. But I don't know what she said she was sorry about.

She looks the same to me. Except for her belly. It sticks out like a big egg and makes her look like she doesn't know if she should sit or lay down so she's always somewhere in between. She rubs it all the time too.

It moves too. The baby inside her I mean. Like a fish that doesn't know which way to swim. She put my hand on it. "It's kicking," she said. "What do you think about that?"

"Mine didn't move," I said.

"Didn't get this big."

"I hate it," I said.

She bought me a dress and shoes for the wedding. They're kind of silvery pink—mauve she calls it. Everything will be mauve, her dress, the flowers. Except the men's suits—they'll be black. She put a piece in my hair so she can fix it like hers because I asked her to.

Barbara said I'll stand next to her just like Reverend's twin will be standing next to him. He'll hold the ring, I'll hold the flowers. And we'll walk in when a lady begins to sing.

We practiced at Reverend's church—that's where the wedding's going to be. There's only a few houses around where the church is. No stores except for a big almost white one down the street from it that some men were working on. There's mostly factory-looking buildings with no names except one that says SILVERCUP and has a huge loaf of bread that also says SILVERCUP sitting on top of its roof. It smells like bread around there too, like it's cooking in the oven—sweet dough and butter and yeast. And it makes the air feel warm. I wondered where Reverend's church got its people from and if they came mostly to smell the bread.

Weeds, some of them taller than people, grow up out of the snow where Tabernacle is. Old rusty pieces of cars too. They grow right through the snow just like the weeds. Right through big squatting rusted fences, through the sidewalk and right upside the brown rusty factories that don't have names. Weeds and old rust. They grow right up to the sky and choke the sun except in the little spot where Tabernacle sits.

Tabernacle looks like a little dingy empty store on the outside except that it has a white cross painted on it and TRUE TABERNACLE APOSTOLIC CHURCH painted on one big window where you'd expect to see the words Cigarettes and Milk—where you would expect to look inside and see counters and salt pork and sugar. EVERYONE WELCOME is painted on the other window where Incense would be. I had to squint to read the songbook because the sun poured through those windows. Too bright. But it kept us warm while we practiced.

It's little inside too. The altar's little and sits flat on the floor, not up high like at Saint Agnes. Pictures are little—none of them are of saints and Mary, just pictures of God. No statues either. It doesn't have pews like Saint Agnes, just little rusting fold-up chairs. Twenty-eight, I counted them, lined up in four rows of six and two on each side of the little altar—I guess that's where Reverend and someone who helps him must sit. Tabernacle smells like my mattress did when the pee didn't stink anymore, just thick and old. Barbara said the smell is mildew from when the roof used to leak.

The lady who was supposed to sing "One Heart" stopped before her song was finished. No one could hear it for the pounding and sawing outside. So Reverend told us to hum the rest of it in our heads while we walked. I didn't step the way they wanted me to. It was too slow sometimes, sometimes too fast. They shook their heads after a while but nobody got mad or anything. I told Barbara I'd rather just sit in the chairs like everyone else. She said, "You'll do just fine."

I sat in Barbara's car when we got back outside and fixed my eyes, then turned around to watch the men who hammered and sawed on the roof of the big store down the street. I squinted but could make out only one of the gold painted words in its big front window.

EMPORIUM.

Mr. Harper told the Woman to put me in a home.

"I know she's yours and all but you have to think about it for your own good," I heard him say.

"Can't bring myself to do it," she told him.

"What the hell do you mean can't bring yourself!" he hollered. I never heard him curse before. I think the Woman didn't either, they both got quiet.

He fixed his voice the same way he fixes his face and calmly said, "It's just that I can't bear to watch what keeping her here is going to do to you, sweet love. She might be young now but wait and see what happens when she gets older."

"Mr. Harper," she said after a minute, "I believe you brought it up cause Ellen fell with your coat again."

"It's a symptom," he said. "Symptoms are like sores, they fester and grow and I don't like being around when they do."

The Woman didn't answer. I waited for him to say, "It's me or her," but he lowered his voice some more and said, "It's for *us*, sweet love. Do it for us."

She said, "When a dog gives away its young, Mr. Harper."

"It's not the same," he said. "You told me so yourself when you said you never did love her."

"But she's mine and she's grown on me, Mr. Harper." The Woman's voice was a mad kind of low that rose higher. "And now you come to ask me to push her aside cause you don't want to see me with her. Just like you don't want to see me with anything else that's mine. Just push and push till I don't have anybody. First no sister, now it's Ellen. Next it'll be Marcus and after that it'll be no husband to see after me. And that won't be good enough, you'll push on till I don't even have my own self!"

"Forgive me," Mr. Harper whispered. "It's just—"

"It's just that I'm sick of you pushing, Mr. Harper." The same mad low voice came back. "I'm sick of not cussing. Sick of sitting up under you every day and you telling me the way *you* like things." Her voice grew loud again, then lower like a song building up and coming down to end. "Sick of you smiling and calling me that shitass name you call me, and your too-tight too-slick shoes and your proper talk!"

The kitchen door slammed open and knocked me into the wall. Mr. Harper rushed past me then turned and said, "Young lady, get my coat."

I stayed against the wall.

"Shit!" he mumbled.

"You know what makes me the sickest?" The Woman's song followed him to the closet and out the door. "It's that smell of yours!"

The Woman doesn't say much to me. Doesn't call me dear anymore either and I'm glad. She's smoking her cigarettes again too. I think she smokes more now. She says, "Ellen," like she has something to tell me, then says, "Never mind, go do something with yourself," and I cut through the alley to help Barbara and Reverend with their new baby. They named her Andrea after the one that's gone. Andrea Renea. Not Elizabeth. They said Elizabeth belongs to me.

The Woman watches me when I cut through the alley to Barbara's. I first saw her do it a month ago—pulled the kitchen curtain back just far enough to see me. I didn't see the rest of her, just the eyes and I knew they were hers.

"Food's cold, Ellen," was all she said when I came back. It's been like that ever since. Eyes at the window, not much said, just something about the food or "Wash the dishes, Ellen."

Except the other day she said, "Just *like* you, Mama, wanting to leave me," when I came back from Barbara's.

I hold Andrea the whole time I'm at Barbara's and I try to decide if I like her. I like the way she feels and smells but I think about them taking her out of Barbara like they took mine out of me and she looks ugly to me sometimes.

Barbara knows when I think that way. She eases the baby from my arms and says, "It's not always that way, Ellen."

She tells me that to remind me of what she said about when she laid with Reverend and got pregnant. "Loving relations," she calls it. "It's when people are together."

"But what about the Husband and the Woman?" I asked her.

"*Loving*, that's the difference," she explained. "It's when both people love each other."

"But what about what they did to you," I asked when I saw them take her baby out of *me* in my head.

"It's what they *did to you* when you didn't want them to do it. When you didn't even *want* it to be inside you. That makes it ugly." She said each word carefully. "It's how they *help* you when you want to have it. When you want what's inside you. Then it's beautiful to you."

"That's why *I'm* ugly too."

"What did I tell you?"

"Well it's why I'm ugly to the Woman then."

She looked at the floor. "Guess so," she whispered, "but we don't see through her eyes." She cut the thick silence. "Do you see it that other way now?"

I told her no and she studied me to make sure, then put the baby back in my arms. I thought about her name, Andrea, and she looked all right to me.

Aunt Della's back. I'm not glad about that. But the Woman is. She's talking more now, so I guess it's okay. Aunt Della doesn't boss her as much, the Woman won't let her. Aunt Della kind of tiptoes around what she wants to say. When the Woman decides it's not what she wants to hear she says, "Della hush," and Aunt Della shuts up just like that. Most of what the Woman wants to hear from her lately is nothing. But she's happy with her here, says, "Della, you just *feel* right," after she makes her shut up.

The Husband stays out of both of their ways. I think he found out about Mr. Harper. I heard him say, "At times a man needs to have a talk with his wife and this is the time," to the old man next door. But when he said the same thing to the Woman she said, "Don't come to me with no mess," and he didn't mention it again until last night after Aunt Della left.

He eased up behind her with his Bible.

"A wife shall forsake all others . . ." he began.

The Woman rolled her eyes upward, then said, "Don't go looking for dirt cause it ain't any."

He tried again. "It says here in chapter—"

"And I'll forsake *you* if you start that shit again."

"Just tried to remember something for Bible study," he said.

~

I don't like the new school. The walk there is about two miles Marcus said. He's good at measuring things. It's not the same as walking to Saint Agnes, Clarissa. There's no grass or weeds to step on. Not much sidewalk, nothing much to look at either along most of the way. Just huge wire fences stretched around smoked-up factories, some still making smoke, others just stuck in soot like the air.

The new school's next door to an empty machine parts facto-ry. That's what the sign on the fence says: —GTON MACHIN— PARTS, EST. 1907. The beginning of the name is missing, so is the E in machine. So is the E and the J and the rest of the name on the sign in front of the school. —AST —UNIOR HIGH, it reads.

It looks like a factory too except it doesn't have a fence or smokestack. It doesn't have little flowerbeds or grass either like at Saint Agnes. No church or convent where the teachers live—nobody lives near the new school. No posters in the win-dows. Most of the windows are too full of soot to see out of.

Some have been cleaned but are beginning to smoke up again.

The new school is huge and noisy and has about a thousand people at least. Makes me really miss Saint Agnes. Its red brick and pretty curved windows matched those on the church and the rectory. Saint Agnes was much smaller too, about the size of the church even though it had all twelve grades. The new school has only three grades. Marcus said that's because it's a junior high. He doesn't like it either. I couldn't find him until we were halfway home.

We don't wear uniforms. Don't have to stand when the principal comes in the room either, don't even have to stop talking or stand when we talk to the teachers. We have a lot of them, one for every subject and a main teacher named Mr. Benjamin who's our English teacher too. He's old and acts like he's already tired of us. There's a room for every subject. Mr. Benjamin tells us which ones to go to for what and we walk around looking for them all day. That's why there's always kids in the halls I guess.

He said, "First period's art in room such and such. You go to geography second in room so and so. You come back to this room for English, then go to math in . . ."

I waited after he finished, then raised my hand.

"You need something?" he asked.

I stood.

"Where do we go for religion?" I asked.

He put on his glasses and looked at me.

"Church," he said.

They laughed.

I did all right until I couldn't find the math room. Everyone I asked acted like they didn't see me, Clarissa. They kept walking and talking to each other. Except a big girl who looked about grown and mad at everybody. She showed me where the room was, then turned and said, "You're the girl was pregnant by her daddy that time."

~

Barbara won't press my hair yet.

She said the sore in my head should have healed by now. She said it should stay clean so she cut the hair around it so that the hair won't get it dirty. I asked her to put one of her pieces over the little bald spot, but she said it has to breathe so it can heal. I found the piece that I wore to her wedding and pinned it over the spot anyway. The Woman said it looks like I have a dead rat on my head.

The Woman's sick again. Last night was the fourth night. She sits up in bed and rocks while she holds her side and hums. All night. And she calls me all night. It's been "wet me a towel," then "go warm up some of my tea, help me out of this bed."

She told Aunt Della she believes it's something Mr. Harper left.

Aunt Della took up for him for the first time. She said, "He was a sonofabitch, I'll give you that, but he ain't been back in going on seven months."

"That man's smart," the Woman said. "You don't know how he might have planned on making it work."

The Woman's letting her hair grow. The Root Worker told her to—said it's strength. She gave her rice in a little cloth bag and some leaves for her sickness. That's what the Woman makes her tea out of.

The Root Worker told her what to do for Mr. Harper too, said it would give him running feet if he sneaked back to do something. Running feet's a sickness that makes people run away, then run themselves to death she said. It will make a person run when he doesn't even want to because he can't help it. And he'll run to wherever it is that you want to get rid of him.

"Throw it over a cliff," she said, "he'll keep running toward the cliff and won't have sense enough to stop. He'll throw himself right over and land at the bottom near the running feet. Throw it in the river, he'll run himself into it."

"Act like you want to get back with him," she said, "and call him out to talk in your yard. Stand in some sandy dirt where he'll get some in his shoes. Tell him you'll clean it out for him, then dust it into here." She handed the Woman a little brown box that said Bulova.

"When he leaves mix it with red pepper then tape it shut. Take it out to Belle Isle and throw the whole thing off the bridge."

I haven't been inside the Root Worker's emporium. The Woman's only been twice. "Familiar just *feels* better," she said when Aunt Della asked why she still goes to that dark old flat. "Just need to feel some things," she told the Root Worker. I think it's because her mother's picture still hangs there.

~

The big girl's name is Tanya.

She's not big in a fat kind of way, just has wide shoulders and big titties. She's in eighth grade like us, Marcus said. He thought I knew her. Aunt Della's friends with her family he said. And James used to hang around over there. The Woman knows them too, but not as well as Aunt Della does.

"I still don't know her," I said.

"Puddin and Mr. Jean—lives in the gray house down the alley and has a girl about ten," he reminded me.

"Don't remember *Tanya* though," I said.

"Cause she runs away a lot," he said. "That's why she's still in eighth. She misses school when she runs away and they keep putting her back."

Maybe that's why she stays mad all the time.

We sit at the same table at lunch always, just Tanya and me.

We don't say much, just sit there and wait for the bell most of the time. Sometimes we do homework. It's easy for me but Tanya has a hard time reading. I asked if I could help her and she said, "You have enough troubles of your own to worry about."

I don't know what troubles she was talking about.

Marcus told the Woman that I sit with Tanya. She said, "Humph! Why ain't I surprised?" Then said, "Thought that girl was gone."

Aunt Della doesn't like Tanya I know. She frowned when the Woman mentioned her and said, "It's your business but from what I heard no child of mine would sit up under her."

"What's it gonna hurt?" the Woman said. "Fruit's already ruined."

Tanya doesn't answer when people talk to her. That's why they think she's mean, besides looking like she's mad all the time. She's really nice I found out. But she only talks when something comes to her mind to say. The rest of the time it seems like she's thinking about something. Like yesterday she said, "I'm tired of you not having anything to eat, Ellen. You want me to buy you something?"

"Half the time you don't have anything to eat either, Tanya," I said.

She didn't say anything else.

Aunt Della's been coming over all weekend. She stays for a couple of hours, then goes home to check on her boys, then comes right back to talk with the Woman about Tanya. I went out on the porch at first while they talked—the Woman said that kids don't have business in grownup's talk—but she called me inside and told me to wash the dishes and listen, I might learn something from hearing what Aunt Della had to tell her about Tanya.

Aunt Della told the Woman that all hell broke loose last week and it was about Puddin and Mr. Jean and what Tanya had done. All the dirt about it got all over the neighborhood she said, because Tanya didn't have sense enough to keep her mouth shut. Nobody's had a thing to do with them since, not even with Tanya's little sister and she wasn't even in the mess.

"Tanya's headed for a no-good end," the Woman told Aunt Della. "Might be best if she was put up in a home someplace . . . I don't know. What do you do with a problem like her anyway?"

"Putting her away's all I can figure," Aunt Della said. "Someplace where she can't get out or run away and do nothing else cause she's too womanish for her own good."

"I don't know, might need to be put up where Odessa is," the Woman said half smiling.

Aunt Della rolled her eyes and squinted her forehead. "That ain't nothing but the devil in you talking," she said to the Woman. And they were at each other again.

Tanya had a baby just like I did, I found out from what Aunt Della said. Only she didn't flush it and Mr. Jean's sister keeps it. Nobody knew too much about it until she had another one.

Everyone thought she had both babies by James. But a lady from the welfare kept coming around and asking Tanya a lot of questions. Tanya got tired and told her everything. Before you knew it they found out that she had the first one by James but the second one it turns out is Mr. Jean's.

It was a big mess.

They came and took Mr. Jean away and he came back the next night and started drinking like a fish. And he's been drinking like that ever since. Mr. Johnson told Aunt Della that he saw Mr. Jean one day peeing in the alley and looking like a bum. Aunt Della said that's hard to believe since Mr. Jean used to be the block club president.

Tanya ran away from home. She came back but hasn't been back to school since. They say that she's running the streets like a whore, only she's doing it with everybody now. For nothing. They say she's still doing it with Mr. Jean too.

Everyone says that Puddin—that's Tanya's mother—is crazy for letting Mr. Jean keep staying there knowing he's laying up with Tanya right under her nose. But some people said Mr. Jean's not to blame because Tanya keeps working something on him so he can't help himself.

After Tanya talked and got Mr. Jean in trouble they found out that Mr. Jean wasn't really Puddin's husband—just lives with them. The Woman said that he's still Puddin's man and that Tanya should have more decency about herself and respect for Puddin than to be messing around with her own mother's man.

"Puddin ought to put something down to keep Tanya away from him," the Woman said. "Don't know about all these young girls nowadays, keeps on enticing these men like they're too hungry to wait—ain't looking at boys no more."

"Don't need to be putting down nothing if they're your own," Aunt Della said. "All you need to put down is a foot. Right up their ass." She looked over at me and I kept washing the dishes like I didn't hear it.

"Wish I did catch one with a man of mine," Aunt Della went on. "Even if he ain't the shit that *yours* is. Much less try and bring something in this world she *had* by him. I'd kill her and the bastard she had it by too. Hear that, Ellen?"

I didn't look up.

The Woman laughed. "Della, leave that child alone," she said. "She ain't been no trouble since God knows when."

I see Tanya every now and then when they send me to the store. She doesn't look like she's fast or anything or even like she works something on Mr. Jean. She just looks a little old to be fifteen and still kind of mad and kind of nice at the same time. She always says, "Hi, Ellen," when she sees me. I want to ask her if she's coming back to school. I miss sitting with her.

I say hi back to her but keep walking when I say it. I don't want the Woman to find out that I've been talking to her. She already says, "You're just like Tanya. That's why she was your friend," when she thinks I want a man to do something to me. She's been thinking that a lot since Aunt Della told her about Tanya.

Tanya's front teeth are gone.

Aunt Della said that Tanya woke her up early yesterday morning banging on her door and screaming that Mr. Jean was trying to kill her. She opened her door and found Tanya standing on her porch in nothing but those little shorts she wears now. No brassiere or shirt or anything. She cried and held one of her eyes like it might fall out. And her mouth bled too.

Tanya told Aunt Della that Mr. Jean came home drunk and cussing and hollering about how Puddin's nothing but half a woman since she can't bleed anymore. Then he started pulling on Tanya but she told him that she'd never let him do it again.

Mr. Jean went into a fit. He cussed and said he knew about her liking a boy named Tyrone who lives around the corner, who's about sixteen or seventeen. That he knew it was why she wouldn't lay with him and he'd kill her *and* the boy and think nothing of it because she was nothing but a whore to him anyway.

Puddin came into the room and told Mr. Jean that he had to get out of her house. Mr. Jean pushed Puddin down, then grabbed Tanya and beat her unmercifully and knocked her front teeth out. Said she'll never grin at a boy again.

After all that he still had Tanya. Right in front of Puddin. Puddin didn't do a thing while he did it, just sat on the floor in the same spot where he'd pushed her down and watched and cried.

"Should've killed her," Aunt Della said. "Messing with a

young boy like that after spreading herself all over town and God knows where else. I helped her out though—got her cleaned up and gave her a skirt and that old green blouse of mine to put on. Even gave her a few dollars to go get herself a room till it all dies over. But if I'd have caught her liking one of my boys she'd be dead by now."

I saw Tanya this morning.

She stood outside Ed's barbershop and looked around like she always does. One of the men who hangs out there leaned over her talking. She smiled and said, "Hi, Ellen," then put her hand over her mouth quick.

I said hi and kept walking.

~

Reverend said that Baptism cleans our souls and makes them pure. That's the way our sins are forgiven.

"But what about Confession?" I asked.

"It's Baptism," he said. "It cleanses the soul and washes sin away—but you drive a good argument, *Reverend* Elizabeth. Got a good head for religion."

I go to Confession anyway. And to Mass too when I get a chance. I go to Tabernacle too. Barbara takes me with her sometimes when she asks the Woman if I can come over to help with the baby. I don't know what I think about going to Tabernacle, Clarissa. It's not quiet like Mass. And it's not exactly like the Girlfriend's funeral church either. I thought it was at first. They sang a lot and it lasted a long time. But Reverend said it's not the same and in some ways I think I can tell. Most times I'm not sure.

Saint Agnes isn't the same either. Sister's not there anymore or Father Ritkowski.

Gone. I look out at the school next door when I'm at Mass sometimes. Seems like I should be going there the next day—eight o'clock Mass, nine school. But then I see the windows all boarded up, chains on the doors, and it doesn't seem like it was ever our school. Just an old dead boarded-up building like the ones over by the Girlfriend's.

There's not many people at Mass anymore either. The Woman said that's because the new priest is colored. And they don't stand around and talk after Mass like they used to. Kids don't play outside on the steps after Mass either. Everyone just leaves and the church becomes old and dead like the school. I walk around and count the dead things when everyone leaves. School, that's one. Convent, two. Rectory, three. Grass, flowers, confectionery store . . . Only things not dead are me and the weeds that grow where the grass used to be.

The Woman said that's what we are—the weeds.

"And weeds have a way of choking the life out of everything that's good," she said. "That's why anything that amounts to something's gonna leave—Saint Agnes, stores, work—before they get caught up in the weeds and can't. Even the sun's gonna leave.

"Even themselves. Weeds have a way of choking the life out of themselves too. They just have to choke something. But their roots keep growing. Even when the rest of their selves is dead. They just stay in the same place and grow and choke cause they don't have sense enough to get away from themselves."

Everything but the weeds is going to leave she said. And all that'll be left will be us and the ones that come up out of the ground.

The Woman and Aunt Della cleaned me out last night.

The Woman told Aunt Della that I smelled so bad she got sick when I was near her and she couldn't stand it anymore.

"It's just filth," Aunt Della told her. "Must be at it again and ain't cleaning herself behind it."

"Well I better not catch Ellen with a man," the Woman told her. "Or she'd do more than just stink—hear that, Ellen?" she hollered over at me.

"Won't do no good," Aunt Della told her. "Ought to teach her how to clean herself out. You can't watch her all the time. Look at what happened with Tanya. And they were friends so it's no telling how much she might sneak."

"Teach? *Hell!* You crazy! How can you *teach* something like Ellen?" the Woman said.

"Clean her out your own self then," Aunt Della said.

The Woman rolled her eyes at her.

"All right then you tell me what you wanna do," Aunt Della said. "Wanna keep on getting sick till you drop dead from it?"

The Woman slumped down in the couch.

"I don't know what I'll do," she whispered. "All I know is I can't stand it."

"Tell you what," Aunt Della pulled the Woman back up. "I'll help you. Do it all the time anyway when those crippled-up women at the nursing home get to smelling. Don't need to worry about catching nothing, a little bleach'll take care of anything."

The Woman told me to follow them up to the bathroom and I watched Aunt Della fill the enema bag up with water, then pour soap powder and vinegar in it. She went down to the kitchen and came back with the bottle of bleach and started to pour it in too but the Woman said that it might not be such a good idea.

"Won't make no difference. Been used so much till it's as tough as those old boots out there," Aunt Della said. "Need something to choke the smell out, not hide it, else it'll come right back."

She told me to lay down on the floor.

The Woman put the foot pan under me and Aunt Della

pushed the thing up inside me so far I jumped straight up and screamed, but no sound came out. I scrambled to my feet and tried to get away. I turned the doorknob but the door wouldn't open. The Woman pulled me back down to the floor and Aunt Della pushed the thing all the way in again. It stabbed something inside me and I screamed so loud that someone put the toilet paper roll in my mouth.

I thought they were going to pull another baby out but I felt water going inside me instead. Aunt Della told me to hold it until she tells me to let it out. I held it until I thought my insides would burst. I let it out and the Woman cursed.

They filled the bag and did it again.

It itches. So bad it feels like the top of my head and my ears are itching too.

The Woman told me not to scratch because scratching's dissipating, whatever that means. I keep acting like I have to pee so that she'll let me go to the bathroom where I can close the door and scratch.

Last time I went down to the basement so the Woman wouldn't tell me to come out where she could keep an eye on me. And I could scratch as long as it itched.

It was bad at school, worse at Barbara's. It drove me crazy. I scooted back and forth in her chair and moved around trying to get my insides to scratch. But I just couldn't reach it that way. After a while my armpits and the top of my head began to itch too.

I scratched my head and arms and rocked back and forth until Barbara laid Andrea down and came over to me and held my arms tight so I couldn't scratch. She pulled me up and walked me to the bathroom still holding me by the arms.

"Ellen, what's wrong with you?" she asked.

"I itch," I said.

"Where?" she asked and I told her it's where I can't say.

She got quiet.

"What's it from?"

I didn't tell her.

"Been with someone?" she asked and I thought about the Woman saying the same thing, only the Woman didn't ask.

I said, "No, ma'am." I thought she'd get mad like the Woman did but she asked, "What did you put in it?"

I said, "Water and soap. Bleach."

She sucked a *whooh!* from her mouth again and looked at me for a long time before she said, "Why'd you do it?"

"Wanted to clean myself out," I said.

She didn't say anything else, just "Watch Andrea for me" and left in her car.

She came back about a half-hour later with a little white bag. She pulled me into the bathroom and opened a jar that said ointment.

"Put this where you can't say," she said. "No soap, no bleach. Just this."

It stopped itching.


"Pride is always gonna come before a fall," the Woman said. "Been *too* proud if you ask me."

The clippers buzzed over my head and I watched my hair fall into my lap and onto the floor.

"Been strutting around here like you some kind of peacock ever since you been going over to that woman's. Can't half do nothing for strutting. Uglier than sin but still strutting like some goddamn peacock—sit up straight."

Little hair shavings started falling. She went on.

"I said, Lord, give me strength! Child ain't nothing to be proud of and that woman's made her think she's gold." She sat the clippers down. "It's talk she might leave, her and that man."

My stomach pushed down inside.

"She tell you?"

"No, ma'am."

"Well that's what a woman from her church told Della." She poured bleach on a rag and the smell burned my nose. "Said she talked about you too." She waited. "Said she wished she could take you." She stopped and laughed out loud. "Said she thinks she can make something out of you—turn around here."

I turned around. The Woman's eyes were wet and red. She laid the rag down and held my shoulders. "Don't care what nobody try to do, you still messed up. Understand that?"

"Yes, ma'am."

Her fingers dug into my shoulders. "Been *ruined*, Ellen. Don't nobody want nothing that's ruined—turn back around— plus you full of haints and the devil and still piss in the bed." She fingered the sore in my head. "Now to top it all off you got ringworms. All that sound like somebody you can make something out of?"

I scrunched my shoulders. "But it's a sore," I said. "From the time with Mr. Harper's—"

She held the rag on my head and the bleach burned the sore. I gritted my teeth.

"Don't wanna hear nothing with his name in it," she said while she held the rag down on my head. "I'm just talking about *you*. Don't think about going nowhere, cause it won't be. Hear me?"

"Yes, ma'am."

"Going off someplace. Just what *she* did, and where is she now? Laying up in a grave someplace I ain't never seen. *Make something out of you*. Funny, those very same words came out of *her* mouth. Got to make something out of my life, she said and walked off with somebody too. Made something all right, a mess out of mine. That what you wanna do?"

I opened my mouth to say no ma'am but she went on before I could say it.

"Chinch bugs. Burned a good mattress cause you had chinch bugs eating you." She laughed. "Nothing want ruined fruit *but* a bug, Ellen. Seems like everything I have is ruined—you, my husband, this hell-hole I live in—but it's mine just the same. Can't even have that in peace without somebody wanting to take it from me."

She took the rag off my head and put lard on the sore. And she put cornstarch on top of the lard, then tore a piece of one of the sheets that Aunt Della had given her, and tied it on my head.

The burning stopped.

"It's Barbara this and Barbara that," she mumbled to herself. "Ain't had no business letting that heifer keep her hands in your head, don't care *who* her husband is. For all I know you been going over there to lay up with him. *Reverend.* Humph! Still a man ain't he?"

"Yes, ma'am."

"You been laying with him?"

"No, ma'am."

"*Make* something out of you," she mumbled. "Now you tell me, how can you make something out of what it ain't?"

"Ellen!" Barbara called from her fence.

I lit the bleach rags in the oildrum.

"Ellen!"

I ran inside and held the door.

"Why'd you cut off all your hair, Ellen?" someone asked.

I cut my eyes at the girls who stood around me, then at Marcus who acted like he didn't see me.

"Cause—I'm really a boy," I said.

"Then why'd they name you Ellen?"

"Cause—it's really *Al*-len. They didn't know how to spell it right so they spelled it like a girl's."

"Then how come you wear girl's clothes all the time?"

"Cause I'm not from here. I'm from . . . Saint Louis."

They laughed.

# DISAPPEARANCES

I PUT MY COAT OVER MY HEAD AND PAID FOR THE WOMAN'S cigarettes, then scrunched up and hurried toward the door.

"I thought that might be you, Ellen," Barbara said to the back of my coat.

I didn't turn around.

"It's real cold outside," she said.

"Yes, ma'am," I answered.

"Well, your head is a fine place to put your coat on a day like this," she laughed. "Think you should put it on before you go outside?"

"No, ma'am. I like it this way."

"It's more than a month now," she said. "Past time for you to visit."

"Don't want to," I whispered.

"Humh?"

"I don't want to see you anymore," I snapped.

"Then at least come by to see Andrea. She misses you."

I ran out of the store.

I'm disappearing, Clarissa.

I've been concentrating and thinking my insides away, a little bit at a time, just like I used to concentrate and make it to Glue. It's a sin to kill myself, I would go to hell for it just as if I had killed another person. But it's not a sin to keep disappearing until you become nothing.

Nobody can figure out how I'm doing it, not even the Root Worker.

The Woman takes me to the emporium every time more of me disappears. I don't mind. I just think about all of the whiteness there—white walls, chairs, floor. The big marble altar—white. And the Root Worker's robe, a flowing white sea. It becomes Barbara's white house and the white store and I become one of the white mannequins—still. And then I concentrate until the whiteness swallows me.

The Woman knows when I do it but she doesn't know exactly what it is. She calls it going somewhere. "Where do you go all those times?" she asked me.

"Nowhere."

She said the Root Worker told her she could tell I'm not there because she can't see anything in my eyes. "Now where do you go?" she asked again.

Still I answered, "Nowhere."

When enough of me isn't disappearing fast enough I eat laxatives and drink a lot of coffee until everything comes out of me.

The Root Worker gave me some stuff this morning, supposed to help she said. It came right back out as fast as it went in. She mixed some more stuff with something sweet and hummed over it, then gave it to me to drink. That came out as fast as it went in too. Finally she told the Woman that the haints are in me again and they had taken over my whole self. She told her there's nothing that can be done except wait to see what happens and that I might die from so many being inside me. There's nothing that can be done about me dying, she said. It's the haints' way of leaving this earth because it's time.

She gave the Woman a number to play and told her that she needs a hit bad because she'll need the money—at least I'll have a decent burial.

I laughed about it, Clarissa. The Root Worker had all those candles and altars and made me drink all that stuff but she didn't know that I was disappearing. I laughed right in front of her and the Woman. I laughed so hard that I laughed and cried at the same time and my sides hurt.

The Woman slapped me. And she did it again and again and said, "I'll slap you to the other side of silly if you don't quit."

I laughed and she hit me. I didn't even try to make it to Glue. Being nothing is Glue.

I miss the mattress.

At least it soaked up *some* of the pee. But the plastic makes me sweat and I wake up soaking wet with pee and sweat and it stings. The smell never goes away, not even when I take a bath or stand outside. It comes out of the inside of my skin and out of my head too.

I wrapped the blanket around my whole head and body one night last week, trying to let it soak up some of the pee and sweat. The Woman whipped me when she found out what I had done. Now I try to hold the blanket away from me so that nothing gets on it. But it still stinks so bad I have to put it out on the porch to air out.

I stay tired. I know you must be tired too, Clarissa. You've become nothing so much that I can't see you anymore. But I keep talking to you so you must be here.

I don't bother to go to Confession anymore. I don't care about hell. To hell with hell. I don't pay attention in school anymore either and I don't care about church or God. And when I look in the mirror I can still see myself but I see a pagan baby first.

I cursed God.

They say that if you curse God you'll have bad luck and He'll strike you dead. But we already have all of the bad luck we're going to have without cursing Him and I wanted Him to strike me dead. So I cursed God.

I cursed the Father, I cursed the Son, and I cursed the Holy Spirit, and I laughed when I did it.

I cursed the haints. I cursed the Woman and the Husband. I cursed Barbara and Reverend, the Root Worker, Marcus, James. *And* his soul. I cursed the grass, the plastic, the plates—I cursed everything I could think of. I even cursed you, just to be doing it. And I cursed myself for running out of things to curse. Then I went to sleep and waited to die.

Nothing happened. Nothing, because that's the way it should have been. I thought about the glop, the thing I had that was supposed to have been the baby that I didn't have. The thing that disappeared as soon as the toilet sucked it up.

*Schloop!* Just like that. Nothing. And just like that I became as nothing as you and the baby are.

When nothing curses, God won't strike it down.

The baby that I had cries.

Sometimes it screams, Clarissa—from purgatory.

I heard it cry and scream again in my sleep last night. The Woman came into my room and woke me up. I pulled the plastic away from my face—tears and sweat had made it stick.

*I* was crying.

The Woman told me that if I cried again she would really give me something to cry about.

"Hold me," I cried. I don't know why. But I wanted her to hold me and rock me as if I were the baby. The Woman looked at me like I had gone completely crazy and bit her lip. I got ready for her to hit me but she just shook her head.

"Lord help you," she said to me sadly. "You've gone off and lost all your sense this time."

I balled the blanket up and held it tight and rocked myself. I pretended that it was the Woman and that she was holding me and rocking me back to sleep.

The baby stopped crying.

I search the mirror all the time now looking for myself to have disappeared in the same way that I used to search the windows for you, Clarissa. It gets hard sometimes. It's just like being chased by the Woman and trying hard to make it to Glue only to look down and find that I'm still standing here on the floor. I looked again and the pagan baby stared back. I knew that it was really me just looking like one.

The Woman hasn't shaved my head in a while so the little prickly porcupine-looking needles that used to be on my head's turned into patches of beady nap balls that are so full of lint it looked like I had a head full of gray and black dust.

My eyes don't bulge like the pagan babies' eyes do in the pictures but the skin under them hangs and makes them look like they would puff up and bulge if someone put a little water on them. My stomach doesn't bulge like the real pagan babies either. And I'm glad. How can I disappear if my stomach bulges? And my legs—they're getting so skinny now that Marcus said they look just like pencils.

My titties are disappearing the fastest. They've shriveled up almost flat and they're beginning to wrinkle up and remind me of the old lady's next door.

I looked at my titties again and laughed.

If Mr. Julius could see me now!

I clean myself out all the time.

I don't use soap powder like Aunt Della and the Woman did. Or bleach. Barbara said I can't use them. But I use vinegar, she said that's okay. And when the vinegar's gone I use plain old water.

The Woman told Aunt Della how I've been cleaning myself out. Aunt Della laughed and said that either I think I'm so nasty I'm trying *too* hard to get clean or I must be laying around a lot. But I just keep doing it so that all of my insides will wash away.

I keep cutting my hair off too, with the clippers, so there's less of my head that needs to disappear. Most people have gotten used to it so no one says anything about it anymore. My head gets cold but that's all right. Maybe the cold will shrink it so it can disappear faster.

~

Barbara was at school. I know she was there because of me.

She talked with Mr. Benjamin in the hall at first. Then the principal walked up. Mr. Benjamin came in and wrote an assignment on the board and they all left together. Everyone knew that something was serious so we kept our heads down and did our English.

Mr. Benjamin stayed with them for a long time, even after the bell rang. We put our things away and went to our next class without anyone telling us we were dismissed.

All I thought about all day was Barbara.

*Barbara came back to school and said that I wasn't myself but was really the baby that she had lost disguised as me. She told Mr. Benjamin that I belonged with her and Reverend, not in purgatory with the baby*

*I had and with James and the other souls. That's when I found out that school was purgatory, why it always feels like a fog.*

*Mr. Benjamin said she couldn't take me if she didn't have proof that I was hers.*

*"But I do," she said. "It's the water that's proof."*

*"What?" he asked.*

*"The water," she said. "It's how deep the water is."*

*She pulled a long skinny weed out of her pocket and it turned into a stick. She used it to scrape away the skin on one of my titties and it wasn't a tittie anymore but a faucet. She laid the stick down and turned the faucet. All the stuff that James had put in me came out at first. Then the soap and bleach that the Woman had put in me. Then what I had put inside me. And then it was water. A lot of it—white-blue. Not in ripples or waves but in a slow still steady flow. It filled the room.*

*I thought we would drown, so I closed my eyes. But it covered my feet. It was soft, pillowy, the way clouds must feel.*

*The water kept coming and Mr. Benjamin whispered, "Take her."*

*I felt Barbara's hand, soft like the water clouds.*

Barbara came back to school like I had hoped she would. She looked worried though and she looked away when she saw me, so I acted like I didn't see her. I felt like I was in trouble but I didn't know what it was that I was in trouble about.

On the way home Marcus asked me if I had seen her.

I said no.

He told me that he thinks Barbara works for the welfare or something because they said she works for the county and she looks like the welfare would have something to do with what she did for the county.

"Wonder why she was talking to Mr. Benjamin?" he asked.

Barbara walked into the room during the middle of our test and Mr. Benjamin told me to go with her to the office.

She was quiet all the way down the long hall, and she walked so fast that I couldn't keep up. I followed a little way behind and noticed a blue spot on the back of her leg. It didn't look like a bruise or anything—just a big dark blue spot like someone tried to paint something there. I wanted to ask her if she knew it was there but decided that it might not be a good idea.

The principal looked up from talking to a freckle-faced lady and said, "We were just talking," to Barbara.

The lady smiled at me. "Ellen?"

I looked at the rubber ball on the end of her chair leg. Barbara took my hand.

"Ellen and I need to be alone," the lady said. Her eyes stayed on me.

I squeezed Barbara's hand.

The lady's eyes followed my arm down to my hand that squeezed Barbara's. "It's okay," she said with her smile still fixed in the same place. I thought about the mannequins, about brownish red dots painted around their pink plastered lips, and squeezed Barbara's hand harder. Barbara squatted in front of me and took my other hand. "It's okay, Ellen," she whispered, then left with the principal.

The lady sat on the edge of the desk and nodded toward the chair in front of it. "Why don't you sit there, Ellen," she said.

I stood next to the chair. I didn't want to sit. I wanted to leave.

She smiled and straightened her shoulders. "It's fine if you don't feel like sitting." She leaned forward and crossed her legs. "We're going to talk about ourselves. We'll start with me if you'd like."

"I don't want to talk," I said.

*Especially not about myself.*

But she acted like she didn't hear me and started telling me all kinds of things about herself that I didn't want to know. "My son is away at college," she said. "Been married twenty-four years . . . Vacationed in Florida last year, have you ever been out of

Detroit?" She talked on and I didn't listen until she asked if there was anything else that I'd like to know about her.

I wanted to know about the freckles around her mouth but I just said, "No, ma'am."

"Your turn." She mannequin-smiled and straightened herself up on the desk like she was getting ready for me to recite something.

"Don't have anything to talk about," I said.

"Really, Ellen, I know you must have *something* to share with me." She didn't stop smiling.

I didn't say anything, just wished she would say, "That's okay then, you can leave."

But she waited.

"Start with when you were pregnant, Ellen."

*An empty wagon's gonna come to no good end,* I heard the Woman say. I closed my eyes and saw them take the baby out and a strange sound came out of my throat.

"What's wrong?" the lady asked. Then she asked again and her breath was on my face. I opened my eyes. "Nothing."

She scooted back up onto the edge of the desk and I wanted to hurry up and say that something was still wrong with me and I didn't know exactly what it was. But the Woman was still inside my head. "Nothing," I said again.

The lady fixed her smile back and said that it wasn't fair that I wouldn't share with her after she had told me so much about herself.

"You didn't have to tell me anything and I didn't ask you anything!" I hollered.

She stopped smiling and stood up and smoothed her dress. "That's enough, Ellen," she said. "You can go."

I didn't go back to my room. Barbara waited for me outside the door and drove me home. She didn't say much except, "How did you do?"

"Didn't tell her anything," I said.

Barbara nodded like it was what she had expected.

"You know you have to talk, Ellen," she said after a while. "Someone needs to know."

"You know. Reverend. That's enough."

"But *they* need to know."

"Then *you* tell them," I said.

She pulled over and turned the car off. "I told them but it has to come from you."

I turned my back to her. "There's nothing to tell."

She groaned. "Ellen, you *know* me. I'll take your hand."

I think about Tanya. Maybe they put her away people say. I think about Odessa too, put away. Both of them put away somewhere. I think about them putting me away somewhere too. Somewhere. Seems like nobody knows where it is. Stuck between here and nowhere—the middle, like purgatory. Then sometimes I think the middle might be like Glue.

Barbara said they'll probably *take* me away for a while but I won't be *put* away because she and Reverend are looking into taking me. I think about that too and I like what I think, only I don't like the idea of leaving the Woman. She's not as bad as it sounds like she is when that lady asks me about her. I told the lady that too and she said, "None of you ever think it's as bad as it is."

She said it when she asked about the scars too. "Fell in some bushes," I said at first when she asked. Then Barbara squeezed my hand and I told her about them, about each time, as she pulled my blouse and skirt up to look for more. I told their stories like I had seen each one on television and they all had titles that began with *the time when.* And she wrote the stories in her notebook. They all ended with "It wasn't as bad as it looks," when she said, "Bet it hurt pretty bad didn't it?"

Most of the time she asks about what the Root Worker does.

I disappear when I talk about that. I don't try to but it's just some-thing that I do. I disappear and hear my voice answer the lady sometimes, answer Barbara other times, always from some other place. I hear Barbara telling me to come back and I can tell she's far away but I never come back until I hear the lady breathe and say, "Oh, my Lord!" Then I know she's finished.

I never tell her about you, Clarissa.

"She asked me about the Root Worker," Marcus said.

"Humh?"

"That lady with the freckles—asked me about the Root Worker, Ellen." He stopped and waited for a crowd of kids to pass.

"Gonna be late, Marcus." I squeezed out from between him and the lockers and hurried toward the math room.

He stepped in front of me. "She asked you too and you told."

"Didn't."

"Ellen, she asked if I ever went with Mama when she took you. How would she know if you didn't tell?"

I looked at the floor.

"You know what Mama told us, Ellen."

I sucked in my breath, then turned around.

"Ellen," Marcus grabbed my elbow. "What does the Root Worker do to you?"

I hurried inside the room.

That's what Marcus asked the Woman too. "What does the Root Worker do to Ellen?"

The Woman bit her lip. "What's Ellen been telling you?"

"Nothing," he said.

"Well something's got you thinking to ask all of a sudden."

I held my breath.

"Just that lady—" he looked over at me and stopped.

"What lady?" the Woman asked.

Marcus eased out of his chair. "Gotta go," he said and picked up his books.

The Woman bit her lip. "What did she ask you, Marcus?"

"Forgot."

I picked up my books too.

"What lady?" she asked again but Marcus was already out the door.


"Had no business telling nobody *nothing!*" the Woman said. "Not even so much as what we eat." She bit her lip and squeezed her fingers around the broom. "And it was you that brought it up to her. *You* did, Ellen! Why else would she pick you to ask about us?"

"Don't know," I said.

"Don't know nothing except how to run your mouth. Told you anybody need to know any of our business, tell'm to come see me. But not you! You gotta go and run your mouth so much you get your own self in a mess."

Pee eased out and snaked down my legs.

"And you just sat there with your mouth shut when I asked Marcus," she went on. "Funny, it's what you should've done when she asked you. Don't hear of'm asking nobody else their business—just you and Tanya." She shook her head. "And Marcus going and losing his head listening to you. *Forgot!* Hell. But he still had sense enough to keep his mouth shut. More than I can say for you! They pick the dumbest one out of the whole bunch and you don't have sense enough to tell'm to ask me. Why'd you think they asked you?"

"Don't know," I said.

She sat down and shook her head.

"Asking me about root workers! *Just what exactly is a root worker?* she asks. *How long did you say you've been taking Ellen to this woman?* she asks like I'm too stupid to know I never even told her that. Now how's she gonna even know to ask about a root worker if *Ellen* didn't mention one?"

"Don't know."

She laughed all of a sudden. "Look at you. Piss running all down your legs and you don't know." She laughed and held her side and cried while she laughed, then sat down and put her face in her hands. "Don't know nothing, don't think nothing, cause you ain't nothing!" she cried.

The Woman stands at the window most of the time watching everyone on the street. She says that everyone is watching her. And if someone crosses over to our side of the street she says they're doing it just to see what's going on in our house. When they're in their yards she says they only come outside so they can see in our windows.

She said they're watching because I talked.

She calls me into the front room all day long to tell me to look at them and then asks me if she's right about what she thinks about them. I keep saying yes ma'am to her. And she says, "Ain't that right, Ellen?" when she gets through cussing at them. I want to say no but it seems that it would be like a sin to tell her what I think.

The lady came into my classroom when the bell rang and walked past me, then turned around. I almost ran for the door.

"Hi, Ellen!" she called out. I acted like I didn't hear her and kept walking.

Barbara came in and took my hand before I could get out. "It's okay," she said. "Let's go to the office."

The lady didn't sit on the desk this time, just stood in front of it and looked at me. She didn't have her mannequin-smile either. She made her lips into a flat thin line while she thought about what to say.

"Says she doesn't know what you're talking about," the lady finally said.

She waited.

I looked at her long pointy high-heeled shoes.

"Says she never heard of a root worker either. Asked me what do they do."

"Yes, ma'am," was all I could say.

She looked up at Barbara.

"Ellen, when did the Root Worker say the baby had to come out?" Barbara said the words carefully.

I shut my eyes and my mouth talked by itself. "Before it got much further along."

"And when was that supposed to be?"

"I don't know exactly but she said it had something to do with the moon."

"What did she tell the Woman to use to take it out?" Barbara asked.

"Something she gave her—I didn't see it. It was long, skinny. And some salt and hot water."

"Who did the Root Worker say the baby's daddy was?"

"The Husband's."

"Ellen, you *know* me," Barbara whispered slowly. She took both of my hands. "Tell us what it looked like."

I screamed.

I can't sleep. All these nightmares, Clarissa. People scream inside my head like they're screaming from hell and from purgatory at the same time. Each one screams loud to drown the others out. I want to disappear but I'm too tired to concentrate.

The Woman woke me up I don't know how many times, screaming all of the things she wanted to scream about. "Ain't nobody stutting you!" she screamed. "Just a bald headed stinking pissy-assed whore." She kicked me with each word. Then she left and came back and started all over again. On and on. All night until I just sat in the corner and waited for her to come back in and kick me again.

It was like that the night before too. And the one before that, cursing and screaming and kicking. All the time I just sat always in the same spot while she kicked me again and again. And each time it didn't feel as bad as the time before.

I hurt almost everywhere now. And I keep feeling and squeezing and pinching the places she didn't hurt to make them hurt even more. Nobody else can hurt me in the places where I can.

They say I've cracked up. But I just look crazy from not sleeping and I walk into things sometimes. They say that I answer them like they had been talking to me when they don't say anything at all. But I do hear them. They say that I'm talking to nobody when I talk to you, Clarissa.

I went to sleep for a little while last night. I dreamed that the Woman and the Root Worker chased me with the enema bag because they found out that I had talked. They said they knew the baby I had was really James's and that was why I killed him. They said everyone knows it now because when I talked it came out of my mouth along with the snake that the Root Worker had pulled from my belly. They caught me and the Woman cursed while the Root Worker took the enema bag and shoved the stem first and then the whole bag down my throat for talking.

"Nothing left but us and the weeds that choke us," the Woman cried while I gagged and choked on myself . . .

The Woman acted like it was a nice surprise to see the lady, then frowned. "Don't you know how to ask somebody in?" she asked Marcus while she held the door and asked the mannequin-lady to come in. "Can't keep nobody standing outside like this."

All the while she said, "These kids act like they ain't never been taught nothing."

"Know you must be hungry," she went on, showing the lady into the kitchen. "You work all day, least somebody can do is invite you to the table."

"Don't bother," the lady said.

The Woman kept on like she didn't hear her. "Won't think about letting you leave this house without something to eat. Now let's get you comfortable. Marcus, go get her a chair."

I slipped past them and listened on the basement step. Marcus came down as soon as he gave the lady the chair. He looked like he was in more trouble than I might have been. "It's that same lady," he said to me like I didn't remember who she was.

I just looked at him like he was stupid because that's what I wanted to call him, stupid, but I changed my mind.

I said, "Yeah, Marcus. Ain't that something. The same one."

"You're in some kind of trouble, Ellen. Know that don't you?"

I didn't answer.

We didn't say anything else, just listened while I made out the shape of Argentina in the spider webs that hung from the wall.

"Ellen has so much junk in that head of hers, no telling what she might come up with," the Woman's voice trailed from upstairs. "Never heard of no roots, no root workers, none of that stuff up in her head. She makes stuff up just like she makes up those folks she gets to talking to."

I stopped looking for Argentina and glanced at Marcus. He stared hard over at the wall where the spider webs were and tried to figure out what I had been looking at for so long. I put my head down to keep from laughing at him but he followed my eyes down to the floor too, still trying to find whatever it was that I saw.

"Oh, she didn't tell you about the folks up in her head?" the Woman asked surprised. "Yeah, she makes'm up and talks to'm.

Thinks they're real, right along with all that root worker stuff she told you about."

I couldn't take it anymore. I laughed out loud and Marcus laughed with me but he didn't even know what I was laughing about.

"Shh! Listen," the Woman said. "See? Told you so. That's her down there laughing like she always do, like somebody's talking, and ain't nothing down there but her and the furnace."

We were quiet again.

"Misses who?" the Woman asked. "Got *me* lost now. I don't know any Misses Toulis . . . Oh, *Barbara* Toulis. That her new name? Didn't know what it was—ain't long ago got married. Course I know her. Used to get her to do Ellen's hair, figured fixing her up some might do her a little good but—you mean she told that woman all those lies?"

Marcus nudged me. "Ellen—"

I hit his knee. "Shh!"

". . . so that's how Ellen got to figuring she was pregnant, you see," the Woman said. "All that time around that Barbara lady while she was pregnant. Wished it on her own self so, she got to believe it. Told you, can't tell what's real when it comes from her lips cause most of it's in her head . . . Now, Miss—what did you say your name was? Well, Barbara's a nice woman and all but she ain't staying with her, I don't care what she say . . . Let me tell you something, Miss whatever you said your name was. That woman can't talk about nobody cause she ain't right herself. Laid with that man before he even married her."

It got quiet and I eased up the stairs and into the kitchen.

The lady stood to leave, then let out a breath and said, "It's what's best for all of you."

The Woman stepped in front of the lady and fixed her eyes on hers. "Which ones did you have to leave you, Miss?" she asked through her teeth.

The lady pulled her eyes away from the Woman's. "That's not relevant," she said.

"Which ones?" the Woman asked again, moving so close to the lady she could breathe into her nose. "You tell me which ones and *then* tell me what's best for me and that child."

The lady didn't answer.

"Look, Miss," the Woman said, "when you step through that door, you gonna leave just like the mama that left me, you understand?"

The lady didn't answer, just looked toward the door like stepping through it was just what she wanted to do. She eased back. "I'm sure—"

"Ain't as sure as what I already know and it's this," the Woman's voice trembled. "What won't leave on its own they try to take it away, just like that woman tried to take my husband. Like James was taken away from me." She pulled out a chair and eased into it. "And if that ain't enough they try to run what's mine away, like Mr. Harper did." She fixed her eyes on the mannequin-lady again. "But let me tell *you* something, Miss. When you step out that door you'll be the last to leave cause nobody else will. Includes Ellen."

"Ellen's already gone," the lady almost whispered.

The Woman scrunched her face and nodded toward me. "Like I don't see her with my own eyes."

The lady reached for my hand and pulled me close to where the Woman sat. She put her hands on my shoulders. "Ever take a good look at her?" she asked. "Her eyes, look in them—what do you see?" She didn't give the Woman time to answer. "I'll tell you. It's what I've seen in others like her—nothing."

She said *I'll tell you* the same way that Sister used to say it when she knew we wouldn't know the answer—*I'll tell you. It's om-ni-potent. Enunciate the ni. What's the word? Om-ni-potent.* A laugh started up through my throat.

"Because she's already abandoned you and herself," the lady finished.

*I'll tell you. He said, I'll be with you until the end of time.*

"Gone?" the Woman asked herself more than she did the lady.

The lady squeezed my shoulders. "She's killing herself."

*I'll tell you. It's your soul that lives forever.*

I laughed, Clarissa. I tried to push it back but it came out anyway.

The lady turned me around and looked at me puzzled. "What's so funny, Ellen?"

*I'll tell you.* I laughed and cried at my own thought.

She looked at the Woman for an answer.

"Haints," the Woman said.

"Heaven," I answered.

The Woman stared into me until she found something familiar. "It's Ellen," she whispered to herself. "*She's* the third."

The lady scratched her chin. "Third?"

The Woman didn't answer, just watched me try to pull the laugh back until I was quiet again. Then she said, "All right, if you say it's best, then Ellen can go."

April seventeenth. That's a week and a half almost, Clarissa, then Barbara's taking us with her. There's something like purgatory in leaving. Stuck between sad and happy. Something like it in the Woman too. Stuck, like something wants to come up out of her but can't. Stuck in her eyes that don't look at me but dig through me like they're trying to reach into my belly and pull. But she won't let it come out. Says, "She's already gone," then leaves it there. Stuck.

We're all stuck, Clarissa. Marcus—he said, "Nobody left but me now, Ellen," then said, "So what, now it'll be quiet around here." And the Husband said, "Might be better off now, Ellen," but looked like he wanted to tell me to stay when he said it.

I don't know.

Barbara said that we'll live in Saint Louis—that's where Reverend's new church is. It's a real church building this time, she said. Brick. Real pews. Used to be Episcopalian.

"It's a long way away," I said. And she laughed and said, "It's still on this side of the country, Ellen."

Reverend's already there, Barbara stayed behind to wait for us. It's okay to say us, Clarissa. That's what Barbara said. "The *two* of you," she calls us now. She said, "It's time that we talked about Clarissa," one day when she drove me home from school.

I told her the same thing I always tell her. "She can't come over yet."

"That's what I need to talk to you about," Barbara said. "You'll have to let her go."

I turned and stared out the window at nothing.

"You won't need her anymore, you'll have us."

I crossed my arms and held myself tight, held my lips tight too.

"There's only one of you. I always knew that," she said. She sucked in her breath. "Ellen, it's time you knew it too."

I put my lips close to the window and blew a breath cloud on it. She waited. I wrote a C for you, Clarissa, on it with my finger. We were quiet the rest of the way.

It was like that the next day too—Barbara quiet, me writing in breath clouds on her window. Yesterday she was quiet for a while, then smiled and said, "We bought a new bed for the two of you."

The Woman found Barbara's combs.

She didn't say anything. Just laid them on the table in front of me and picked up her dust rag. I didn't say anything either, just stared at the thread still knotted around the teeth and the dust that covered it. A hum came from under her breath, then her lips moved until it turned into a song. "Oh Lord, don't move this mountain," she sang low at first. I thought about James and her singing grew louder. "Don't take away this stumbling block, but move it all around," she sang while she dusted around me and the combs. She stopped as suddenly as her song did and fixed her eyes on me. "You tell me what it is, Ellen," she whispered.

"Combs," I said still looking at them.

She threw the rag down on the table. "Look at me, Ellen!" she said. "What in hell made you think I got dumb all of a sudden?"

I didn't know what she wanted me to tell her.

"Where'd they come from, Ellen?" her voice was a whisper again.

"Barbara," I said to the floor.

"Barbara!" she laughed. "Oh, *Mrs.* Toulis."

Something pressed down on my insides and it made me feel like I had to pee. The Woman hummed louder and I stood up and wriggled and crossed my legs tight.

She stopped humming. "Better not move," she said and kept kneading the cloth into the table with the ball of her hand. She fixed her eyes into black shiny icicles that stabbed sharp into my knees. The pee eased out warm and snaked its way down into my socks. It became cold like the Woman's eyes.

She picked the rag back up and hummed while she put her weight on it and pressed it into the table. My stomach tied itself up into a knot.

The Woman stopped dusting and put her hands on her hips. "Pissed on yourself, Ellen."

"Yes, ma'am."

"You tell Barbara how you piss on yourself?"

I looked at the floor.

"Tell her about the mattress you ruined?" She moved close and I smelled cigarettes on her clothes. "What about those chinches, Ellen? Didn't tell her about that, did you? Didn't tell her about how you stay in the basement all the time and talk to yourself either. Didn't tell how you smelled like you laid up, how you didn't even have enough decency about yourself to wash what you did off your own clothes either, did you?" She breathed it all into my nose.

"Told her what you wanted to tell and she gave you this shit," she mumbled under her breath. "What kind of mess *is* it, Ellen? What's it gonna do?"

"Huh?"

She picked the white comb up with her rag and held it near my face. A hundred little thread knots poked through the dust web that covered them. "*This* mess," she said. "What was it working?"

"Nothing," I said. "Just knots I tied."

She dropped the rag and comb. "*You* tied'm!" she said like it was the answer to something. "Who told you to do it?"

"Nobody. Just did it."

She stared through me until she recognized something in my face. "Just knew didn't you?" she eased the words through her teeth. "Cause it's what you did to make me sick!"

"But I didn't—"

She nodded. "It's what you did all right. It's what you did to take James away. Didn't want me to have my own child. Did it to take my husband from me too. Didn't want me to have nobody cause you didn't want me. And then you did it to take Death to that woman cause you wanted me to take my own self away like you took yourself away from me."

She picked up the broom and bit her lip. "What did you want me to do that you could have done better?" The ice in her eyes melted into puddles. "Now you want to leave me again like you left me before," she cried. "How can you make me suffer like this?"

She got quiet suddenly for a minute and sat down. Just as

suddenly she jumped up and swung the broom at me. "It was you all this time, Mama!" she screamed. "All this—*you* did this to me!"

I ran out the kitchen door.

"What can you do, Mama?" she hollered after me. "Mama, *please*, you got to fix this mess you made!"

The Woman calls me Mama all the time now and it feels funny, Clarissa.

She says, "Mama, will you brush my hair?" and "Mama, will you go get my cigarettes?" She doesn't *tell* me anymore, she asks. Just those two things all the time—brush my hair, get my cigarettes—except last night when she woke me up and said, "Mama, why'd you do that to James?"

The Root Worker told her to burn the combs. She said pour turpentine on them first, then burn them with my womanhood rag and some of my hair.

"Can't bring myself to burn what's my mama's," the Woman said, fixing a smile on me and taking my hand.

The Root Worker stared at us for a long time, then went over to her altar. She stayed there for a while pouring and mixing. She came back to the table with a jar of thick black stuff that looked like shiny mud and smelled like black drought syrup. "Then we have to put some of this up in her," she said.

I thought about the enema bag and the cold long thing they took the baby out with.

You screamed, Clarissa. Screamed "No!" flying over the table and digging your teeth into the Root Worker's face.

The Woman smiled.

"Did you see what Ellen did?" I heard an old woman ask. I didn't look up, just held the groceries tight against my chest and crossed the street.

*What Ellen did.* That's most of what everyone's talked about for two days now. It seems like the blood from the Root Worker's face must have covered me—red—so that the world would know.

"What Ellen did." That's what I heard Aunt Della say when I woke up this morning. "Couldn't *believe* what that Ellen did!"

"Don't want to talk about it, Della," the Woman said.

"Well you ought to talk about it with somebody," Aunt Della said. "Sounds to me like you got a problem bigger than you might know."

Silence.

"Mama!" the Woman called.

Aunt Della laughed. "Stop calling that child Mama. I swear you getting as off as she is."

"Laziness is a sin before God, Mama!" The Woman hollered. "Should've been up!"

Aunt Della laughed again. "Didn't know a root worker could bleed," she said as I eased into the kitchen.

"Della, even the water bleeds," the Woman said. "Dishes still here from last night, Mama."

I hurried over to the sink and ran the water so that I wouldn't see Aunt Della's stare. But I felt it just the same, right on the back of my neck. It crept into my head where it stayed the whole time she was there. Something else stayed too. Thick and heavy.

Aunt Della sucked her teeth. "Clamped her teeth right into the Root Worker's cheek," she said like she had seen it happen. "That's what they tell me at least. Locked her jaws on it and ripped a big chunk of skin right off."

The taste of the Root Worker's thick skin and blood filled my mouth. I spit in the dishwater but it was still there. I put my head under the faucet and tried to drown it out.

"Della, told you I don't want to hear no more!" the Woman said.

It didn't mean anything to Aunt Della. "Just like a dog that's lost all its sense in the heat."

"Della!"

"Told *me* root workers don't bleed."

"Umh."

"Ain't like it was me that said it first," Aunt Della went on. "Everybody I talked to said it's so. Now, how come?"

"Della, I can't tell you how come," the Woman said. "All I can tell you is what the Root Worker said and it's that Mama's an instrument."

"Mean Ellen? What'd she mean *instrument?*"

"Instrument that the devil or something worse must be using. That's why Mama wanted her blood."

"But a root worker don't *bleed!*" Aunt Della almost hollered.

"Della, *Jesus* bled."

"Wasn't the devil's work though."

"Worse."

Silence.

"Said she ripped a hole in the Root Worker's face?" Della said to herself.

"Clear through to the bone. Could see the yellow—" the Woman caught herself. "I'll be damned, another hole" she whispered. "Tell me *that* ain't worse than the devil!"

The skin taste covered my tongue and then began to come up from my stomach. I held my mouth and ran for the bathroom.

"Mama!" the Woman hollered after me. "I don't see those dishes washed!"

It's supposed to be tomorrow, Clarissa.

The moving truck's already in Barbara's yard. I won't be going I know. The Woman didn't say it but I know anyway. She won't let me out of her sight. Can't go to school, to the store. She won't even let me go to the basement. "Might sneak off," she said.

The Woman's been waiting at the kitchen window most of the past two days—ever since she decided it was Barbara who wanted the Root Worker's blood. She keeps her eyes on Barbara's house the same way she kept them on me when I used to cut through the yard to see her. The only time she leaves the window is to pee, watch me sleep, and to search the cabinets for the can of red pepper. When she found it she tucked it into her brassiere. It's still there, waiting for the rest of the running feet.

The Woman ran out to the porch hollering, "Mama, come out here where I can see you," over her shoulder when Barbara came out to talk to the moving men.

I followed her out to the porch, where she folded her arms and tapped her foot like tapping it would make the men hurry up and leave.

"Now don't you move, Mama," she said when the last man got in the truck.

"Barbara!" she called just as Barbara turned to go back in. "Need to see you a minute!"

Barbara dusted her hands and came over to the fence, untying the scarf that tied her hair.

"Need to talk in the yard, it's private," the Woman said easing closer to the side of the house.

"Morning, Ellen," Barbara called when she came near.

I didn't answer.

"Cat's got her tongue," the Woman said. "Come on back where we can talk." She led Barbara to the side of the house. "You been to Belle Isle?" I heard her ask. "Fine place for a memory, just across the bridge."

"Been there once. Too many cars," Barbara said.

The Woman grunted. "Ain't that many early up in the day. Thought it'd be nice for a goodbye, just you and me and Ellen."

"Kind of cold this time of the year," Barbara answered

slowly. "Ellen, you're the one that's leaving. What do you think?"

I eased to the side of the house and stopped. My eyes stuck on Barbara's feet that sank up to the sides right in the sandy brown dirt where Mr. Harper's had been. "It's running feet," I whispered.

"Told you, cat's got her tongue," the Woman laughed.

Barbara followed my eyes to her shoes. "What's running feet?"

"The dirt on your shoes," the Woman hurried up and answered. "It's what these kids call the dirt on your shoes." She bit her lip and looked up at Barbara. "All I ask for's my own goodbye. Least a woman should get when she gives you her own."

Barbara watched me while she thought. "When?"

The corner of the Woman's mouth eased into a smile. "Sure is a pretty scarf," she said. "Looks like you'd give me that little something."

Barbara took the scarf from her head and handed it to her.

"In the morning about eight," the Woman said fingering the scarf.

Aunt Della said that taking me is a bad idea since I'm the instrument and who knows. The Woman told her that instrument or not it's what her mind tells her to do and taking me is what she's always done since it brings her luck.

I don't know. Seems like a cat really did get my tongue when the Woman said *gives you her own* to Barbara. Something held it, stopped it from moving when I tried to say that running feet's more than just dirt. Tried to say, "It'll run you to your death, Barbara. It's what I think happened to Mr. Harper." But I held it inside my mouth right along with my tongue.

I don't know. Maybe it was the way that she said *gives you her own* that made me say, "I won't leave, you have to believe me!" when Barbara left.

The Woman didn't say anything at first. Just kept sifting the tiny rocks from the sandy footprint that Barbara had left. When only the dirt was left she scooped the footprint into an envelope that said Postage Guaranteed.

We went back into the kitchen, where she poured the sand from the envelope and the red pepper into Barbara's scarf. "Must think somebody's off," she said without taking her eyes from the scarf.

"No, ma'am," I said and tried again. "It's just that—"

"It's just this," she cut in as she gathered up the scarf ends and tied them into a tight knot around the stuff to keep it from leaking out. "What you telling me don't mean nothing except it's what she *told* you to say to make a fool of me."

We stayed up most of the night, the Woman with the scarf and me, too tired to sit up straight. She sat at the kitchen window looking out like she expected someone to come out from the blackness at any time.

I nodded off, then jerked up straight when I caught myself almost falling out of the chair. The Woman still sat at the window. Sleep this time. I made an Act of Contrition inside my head, not for forgiveness but hoping that Barbara would know with a miracle.

I eased out to the side of the house and put my bare feet in the sand. All the while I felt the eyes on me, Clarissa. Felt them in the darkness when I got on my knees to sift the dirt. I looked up at the window. The Woman's head slumped in a nod where she sat. I looked around but except for the little light that came from the kitchen window it was pitch black everywhere. I tipped back inside. The Woman snored.

I still felt the eyes.

I pulled and squeezed, flattening the sand and red pepper that I'd tied in the scarf Barbara had given me a long time ago. I felt the eyes again as I tied thread around the scarf in a love knot so that the sand and pepper wouldn't shift into a lump beneath my clothes.

I watched the Woman sleep until I dozed off too. I woke up and light came in from the window where the Woman still sat, this time hugging a cup of coffee between her hands.

"Got to go pee," I said and tried to stand up but my foot was asleep.

The Woman kept her eyes on the window. "She tell you to say that too?"

"No, ma'am." I kicked my foot and rubbed it until I could feel little needles pricking it back awake.

The Woman stood and stretched. "Well go on," she said and followed me up the stairs.

~

I wrinkled my nose at the smell of fish and early morning dampness that came up from the river. It reminded me of new pee after a long drink of water—too weak to burn your nose, too new to have settled into mustiness. It was quiet except for the pale new leaves that rustled on the old big trees and the lazy sound of the water nearby. Except for the far off noise of cars going down Jefferson to Chrysler. Only a good walk from home, but it felt so far away.

Weeds grow on Belle Isle just like at home, Clarissa. But it seems like the weeds on Belle Isle forgot about choking, just let everything be. Flowers grow up purple and white in the middle of the weeds. So does grass. And trees older than anything I've seen, don't rot and die like the trees did at home—they grow yellow-green moss in their trunks.

I watched a squirrel run by—haven't seen one since I was about six. And a deer peeked out from behind a skinny new tree, then ran away when it saw us. Water weeds crowded tall along the edge of the bridge. They shared the space with sand that had blown from the beach nearby, shared the edge with a squashed cigarette butt, a piece of sandwich, and an old truck tire.

The Woman fingered her bosom and silently pulled me along as she picked her way through the grass and sand. We stopped next to an old ash-gray man who fussed with his fishing pole near the bridge. He didn't look up but asked, "Where's your coats?"

The Woman didn't answer, just waited while he tied a piece of red meat to the end of the pole and stuck it in the water. She stepped closer. "Seen a tall brown-skinned woman?"

He pointed the tip of his pole toward the other side of the bridge. "Over there," he said.

I didn't see anything except some trees and more grass and the foggy buildings on the other side. They were the foggy faraway shadows that I used to see on the way to Saint Agnes. Faraway purgatory worlds, Clarissa. Both of them, just fogs.

The Woman squeezed my hand and we walked to the edge of the bridge. A bird fussed its wings from under the girders beneath our feet. It came out from its hideout and flapped its big gray wings once more before it took off in search of someplace else. It wouldn't come back for awhile, I knew. We had found its Glue.

The wind whipped long red streaks into our naked arms and groaned out loud from its own sting. We held the concrete edge and waited for the wind to leave. It fussed at first, just like the bird, then gave the bridge to us. The scarf had eased its way up from the woman's brassiere. She caught it before it could fall and checked the knot that held the running feet. She stopped and balled the knot part tight in her fist and wrapped the rest of the scarf around her hand. We kept walking until we reached the other side.

The water was thick and brown near the bridge where we stood. Tired limp weeds drifted in it along with bottles, a rag, and old gray sticks. They moved around—the water and the weeds, the rag, the bottles and sticks—but didn't go anywhere, just fussed around like the old man and the bird and the wind. It was what everything on this side did.

There was just ice blue out in the middle of the water. No weeds. No rusted things, no dingy grays. Just clear ice blue water that touched ice blue clouds and nothing else. The water rested under all of the blueness. Still. Everything rested out there. Even the air, quiet. I shut my eyes and made myself as quiet as the out there middle.

The Woman waited for a long time, then cupped her hands to her mouth and called, "Barbara! Now you said you'd be here!"

Nothing.

I looked around. Nothing moved. I breathed relief that Barbara didn't come and a thin gray fog stuck in the air right where I had breathed it.

"Barbara! Over here!" the Woman called and waved her arms.

I looked up. At first I thought she was the Root Worker, Clarissa. She wore a big white dress with gold around the sleeves like the Root Worker wears at her emporium. But then she came closer, carrying a big straw bag. The wind whipped the hem up around her ankles and all I could look at was her high-heels and red toenails.

The Woman fixed a long hard stare on Barbara as though she recognized her but didn't know exactly who she was. I stared too, Clarissa. Up close she seemed like she might have been an archangel with big white and gold sleeves floating in the wind.

Barbara didn't pay our stares any mind just rubbed her arms and looked around, then said, "Might be a little warmer under that tree."

The sound of Barbara's voice snapped the Woman out of her stare. "Just as soon stay near the water," she said as she unwrapped the scarf from around her hand. She squeezed the scarf-ball.

Barbara shrugged, then knelt and unfolded a small white sheet from her bag. She spread it out in front of her. "Didn't bring much, not much of a cook. Heard you are though." She pulled out a cup and a little glass plate.

The Woman smiled. "Easy to fool yourself when it comes to what folks can cook up."

Barbara thought about what the Woman said. "Guess so," she laughed. "Guess we all can fool ourselves about a lot of things." She patted the grass next to her, smiled up at me and said. "Sit on down and keep me company."

I stooped to kneel and the Woman pulled my arm. "Hadn't meant to stay long," she said.

I straightened back up.

Barbara fished around in her bag. "Long enough to give me that running feet?"

The Woman sucked in her breath, then pushed it from down inside her throat. "Running feet?"

"It's in your hand," Barbara said like she thought the Woman didn't know.

The Woman squeezed the scarf-ball tighter. "For a woman all holy and married to a preacher, funny how you know about running feet."

"Used to watch Mama work on more than a few fixes," Barbara answered as though it was a matter of fact.

The Woman bit her lip. "Root worker?"

Barbara shook her head.

The Woman closed her fingers tight around my arm. "Then it was your *mama* who's a cila," she said under her breath.

"A healer," Barbara said standing up.

The Woman nodded. "They call themselves that too." She frowned. "And you're your mama's child. An apple ain't gonna fall too far from the tree you know."

Barbara shrugged. "Maybe not."

The Woman studied Barbara for a minute, then something came to her. "Know about Thomas Stevens don't you?"

"Knew him personally," Barbara answered. "Jessie too."

Silence.

Barbara nodded at the Woman's hand. "That running feet. All I want to know is if it's for Ellen too."

The Woman gave her a puzzled look. "*Came* from me didn't she? Would take the devil to give a thing like that to it's own."

Barbara shrugged. "Ellen's came from *her* too, and she flushed it. Apples don't fall . . ."

Something colder than the wind wrapped around me. I rubbed my arms but the coldness stayed a while longer, then went into the Woman's eyes.

"Ellen ain't at herself!" she frowned.

"All the more reason," Barbara said.

The Woman squinted, then stepped in front of me. "Let me tell you one thing," she said, "can't say I like her, being off like she is. But I won't be the one to cause her death. Ain't like me to kill."

"But you'd kill Barbara," came out of my mouth. It was me that said it, Clarissa, not you. I flinched.

The Woman fixed the ice in her eyes on me this time. "You lost your head?"

"No, ma'am." I had just found my head. Started finding it when I tasted the Root Worker's blood in my mouth. And it was heavy with the tongue that the Woman said the cat had. The cat didn't have it, Clarissa. It was there thick with the Root Worker and the silence that kept my head down.

*Always looking down, Ellen.*

I straightened my shoulders and pushed the silence out. "It's what the running feet's supposed to do." I looked up at Barbara. "Supposed to cause your death."

"She'll cause her own!" the Woman said.

"Never intended to let me take her in the first place did you?" The softness of Barbara's words put a wall between ours.

The Woman frowned. "No more than you intend to let some-body take yours."

Barbara didn't say anything else. Just knelt beside the sheet again like what the Woman said had ended the whole thing and there was nothing else to do but have her picnic before the run-ning feet caused her death. The Woman didn't say anything either, just watched Barbara at first, then me. Studying me. I won-dered at the sound of my voice not blended with yours, Clarissa. Wondered at the Woman's silence.

Barbara pulled a boiled egg from her bag, peeled the shell, and laid it carefully on the little plate. Then she took a jar of water from her bag and poured some into her cup.

The Woman shook her head and looked at Barbara like she might have been crazy. "That all you brought?"

"It's all I need," Barbara said putting the plate back on the sheet. "Ellen?" She pulled a long weed blade from the grass and tied the love knot that she had taught me at the alley fence.

I sat down beside her and took the egg.

"The devil fed Eve too, Ellen," the Woman almost whispered. She frowned, then said the rest, hoarse but louder. "Sent her straight to hell."

I bit the egg.

"Why the running feet?" Barbara asked after it was quiet for a while.

The Woman thought about the question. "Said it comes in threes."

Barbara wrinkled her nose. "It?"

The Woman backed away. "Death. Ain't that what you put on Thomas Stevens? Said you put it on him the same way he did his dirt." She kneaded the scarf-ball in the palm of her hand. "Figure the third ought to be you since you the one that gives it."

Barbara frowned. "All this because of *him*?"

The Woman shook her head. "Don't take me for crazy. *Who*

you take Death to ain't never mattered to a cila and you know it. Just have to take it to somebody cause it's what you *do*." She nodded toward me. "But you see Mama over there?"

Barbara opened her mouth but the Woman didn't give her a chance to answer. "Running feet's so you won't come back and use her to work your death on us."

Barbara wrinkled her brow. "Mama?"

"Ellen. Same thing."

Barbara covered the top of the cup with the little glass plate. "Suppose something stands in the way of me and your running feet?" She pulled a small bottle that said White's Laundry Bluing from her pocket and unscrewed the lid. "Ellen already ate the egg."

She pulled another egg from her bag and eased it into the cup. "This one holds both—my soul and Ellen's now." She poured the bluing on her finger and traced it into a cross on the side of the cup.

*Cause she's a cila, Della. That's what cilas do!*

I imagined my soul was the blue line that her finger left. It seeped through the cup's tiny paint cracks and through the shell of the egg inside. I wondered if that was what a cila must do— save souls.

The Woman didn't say anything, just watched. But Barbara looked up at her anyway and answered the question that she didn't ask. "It's passed to someone else."

The Woman's laugh woke the early quiet. "Should've left the blue for your husband's shirts," she said. "Running feet's already here."

"No, ma'am," I said. "It's sugar."

"Ellen ain't at—" the Woman started.

"Put sugar in the scarf when you went to sleep," I said.

She turned around and fixed a look on me that wasn't exactly mad but a question that might turn into mad.

I pushed on. "Poured the other stuff out."

The Woman glanced from Barbara to me.

I reached inside my skirt and pulled out the scarf and held it up. "Gave it to myself."

"Have mercy, Lord," the Woman whispered. "Ellen, you don't know . . . What got into you?"

I didn't take my eyes from hers.

The Woman scratched her head. "Ain't like you," she said to herself over and over as her eyes searched mine for an answer.

She suddenly nodded and smiled. "Just *had* to find a way to run from me again didn't you, Mama?" She lifted her dress and wiped her face with its hem. "All my life all you ever did was run. Run to your grave wasn't enough so you steal your own self some goddamn running feet!" Her lips pulled back into a tight grin that twisted thick long veins up into her neck.

She snatched the scarf and waved the knot in front of my nose. "Ellen might not be much but I'll be damned if you take her to her death!"

I saw *Ellen* then, Clarissa. She peeked out at me from inside my head. Then from Mr. Julius's store window—purple and blue. I squeezed my eyes shut. But she looked out at me just the same. From the Root Worker's place—nose filled with the smell of turpentine and candlewax and womanhood, mouth full of skin and blood, pee and silence. Eyes full of nothing. The silence and nothing began to swallow her. And it sucked me in with her.

I opened my mouth wide and spit. "No, ma'am. *I'll* be damned if I stay!"

The Woman's whole face knotted. "Means you'd just as soon take hell."

"Just as soon," I said.

"Then you take her," she whispered to Barbara. "Take my crazy child, hear me?" She hugged the scarf. "Soon as see her with the devil than see her dead."

I turned around and looked through Barbara's glasses into the same eyes that had watched me sift the rocks from the sand the night before.

She read my thoughts. "But you ate the egg," she said.

"Yes, ma'am," I answered. "Something to do with saving me?"

She nodded. "Healing you."

I looked back at the Woman. She turned from me, her shoulders stooped as she walked away to kneel beside the water.

"I'll come back to see you—" Something stuck in my throat. I tried hard to push it out but it wouldn't budge. I looked at Barbara.

"It's okay," she said.

"Mama," I whispered. I watched the Woman's shoulders tremble then stop. "I'll come back soon, Mama."

# EPILOGUE

The Woman is old, Clarissa.

Tiny and frail, stooped and gnarled way beyond her sixty-nine years. She stares out from behind half-drawn yellowed curtains at the world she has abandoned, waiting patiently for her turn to die.

"She's been this way since you left," Marcus said to me. A shadow crept into his eyes, then disappeared behind a mask that grinned as he mocked indignant. "You were stuck on Glue a long time, Ellen."

I smiled at the memory of the game and at the sadness of a nearly fifty-year-old man who could only wonder about a life outside of the one that he was born into.

*And you were stuck here*, Marcus, I wanted to answer. No family to call his own. No memories except the ones trapped inside his childhood.

"And what about you, Marcus?" I asked instead.

He glanced over at the Woman. She sat quietly at the window, tracing her fingers over a faded dog-eared picture. "She got it for you, you know."

"Humh?"

"Day after you left, she got that picture back. 'It's all I have left of her,' she told the Root Worker. 'Seventy-five dollars,' the Root Worker said." He shook his head. "Oh, it got to her, but she let it go and said, 'Well, if I have to pay for what's mine,' then paid her with the light bill money." He laughed. "Used candles a long time—"

"But that's not *me*, Marcus," I interrupted.

He eased the picture from the Woman's hand and held it up to my face. "So what's the difference, Ellen?"

The Woman's mother stared out from the picture, a remarkably ten-years-younger version of me.

*So what's the difference?* I said to myself when the Woman asked, "What took you so long, Mama?"

I had just stumbled on the word *mama*, looking for a name other than the Woman to call her.

*So what's the difference*, I thought, then cradled her and answered, "Hush, baby, I'm here now," with a twinge of envy that she could say the word that I could say only one time. The memory of when I last said it grew huge inside my head then twisted around my insides. It pushed the memory of my last visit to the Root Worker's—black and muddy—from where I had buried it. I tried to shut it out, but it oozed into my head anyway. Just like the dark shiny turpentine-and-black-drought syrup-smelling stuff at the Root Worker's. This time, though, I didn't scream. I choked on it.

"But she sacrificed herself for you—in her own way," Marcus said, like he could see what I remembered. "She might have been gone, but she thought she had saved you." He shook his head. "Mama gave the Root Worker all that she had for this picture." He laughed. "Would have milked the Death thing until she was dry, too. But Mama wasn't afraid anymore." He closed his eyes to bring the day back.

I shut my eyes too, to see it.

"Said she'd just as soon wait than fear." He took the picture from me and slipped it back between the Woman's fingers. "Next day, she went into herself and waited to become the third death. Still waiting."

I tried to plait a piece of her tangled hair. *Need to get Barbara to do it*, I thought. "But the Husband?"

"We took care of his burial ourselves—me and Aunt Della. Never did tell Mama. Thought it would be best that way."

He smoothed down the clump that my feeble attempt for a plait had made in her hair. "Thought about putting her away a couple of times," he said, "but then I thought about Aunt Della's Odessa . . ." His voice trailed off as his shoulders began to slump into a stoop like the Woman's.

"Aunt Della?" I asked more in an attempt to bring Marcus back than out of curiosity.

He pulled his shoulders back with himself. "Died. Last year. Think it might have been cancer." He chuckled. "Never did see about it, said she'd rather have a lump than a hole. It's just us now, Ellen."

Funny, I had expected to see some of the Husband in Marcus, but he's more like you, Clarissa. Tall and somewhat wiry. His beard, peppered with more gray than he has on his head, gives an odd sort of handsomeness to his still crooked-toothed smile. And like you, he's thoughtful to the point of sacrifice. It saddens me to think that this is all that most of his life has been.

It was twenty-eight years ago when the Husband passed away. Twenty-eight years. They said it was a heart attack. Marcus believes it was more of a broken heart, although he's not quite sure what it was that made the final break—losing me or losing the Woman to the death she had chosen.

Marcus was full of all of the spirit and dreams of a nineteen-year-old then. But his dreams were shelved by the Woman's needs, and his spirit faded along with her outbursts. He became content to just be.

Until I told him about you, Clarissa.

It seems to have sparked a longing for the life he's missed and a curiosity about the world he's never seen.

"A daughter," he says shaking his head every now and then. "You say she's *how* old?"

"Going on twenty, Marcus," I pretend exasperation at answering the question at least a dozen times.

"Where'd you say she's studying?"

I tell him Massachusetts, and he scratches his head like I had said the moon.

"Her name's Clarissa," he repeats, then wonders why it sounds familiar.

Just as curious to him is the idea of Saint Agnes opening as a secular school and me teaching there. "*You*, Ellen. Never would have thought." He laughed, then said, "It's gonna be work."

Marcus doesn't mind the work though. He's at Saint Agnes before the work crew sometimes, putting up drywall, chopping down weeds. It's smaller than I remembered. More ragged and dingy than I had imagined. Crumbling like the leaning stick houses around it. But your grandfather once said that, as long as the foundation's good, it's salvageable.

I thought, "Yeah, it's salvageable," as I looked out the window at a little girl with tiny plaits who hollered "Glue!" as she jumped on the weeds where grass once grew.

# ACKNOWLEDGMENTS

WITH THANKS TO THE MANY PEOPLE WHO MADE THIS BOOK possible: Amanda Materne, Albert DePetrillo, Robert E. Jones, Tracy Carns, and Bruce Mason, who came into my life as agent, editors, publisher, and publicist, and remain in it as special friends. To Arielle Eckstut, Miek Coccia and James Levine Communications and The Overlook Press for believing in it. To Virginia Law Burns, Linda Gross, and Frances Kuffel whose advice helped me along the book's journey. To Hannelore Hahn and the International Women's Writing Guild for providing an environment where creativity can grow.

Special thanks to my friend and confidant, Doug Evans, who was there for me when the chips were down and who told me to write, which started it all in the first place. To Howard Hull, my lifelong friend who provided a computer, tolerance, and moral support. To Jeannetta Holliman, my spirit sister. We shared houses, children advice, and ideas through the the book's entire conception and birth. To George Holliman who provided support and tolerance along the way. To Deborah and Larry Warren for being like family. And to Chiquita Lee and Rodlyn Douglas for long night talks and inspiration.

Thanks to my sons, Melvin (Tiran) Gore and Raymond Burton, for being my conscience and my spirit. To my daughter-in-law, Teresa Gore, the keeper of the flame. Thanks to my long-time friend, shaman, and mentor Peter Friedlander, who taught me to see beyond the familiar, and to Stuart Henry who sees beyond the impossible.

Thanks to my lifelong friends Marcella Wright and Regina Burnett for sticking by me when others gave up, and to Regina's sister, Gwen, for believing in this book before it took shape. And thanks to my brave newer friends who have no fear of wild ideas: Ballerie Allen for sharing her books, ideas, and family; Paulette Davis for friendship, support, and a good cup of coffee; Gerri Stone whose poetry lifts me like a good cup of coffee; Angela Wynn who keeps me grounded when I need to be; and to my newest friend, Elizabeth Buzzelli, for wisdom and sanity when the world gets foolish and crazy.

Thanks to all of my Guild friends whose spirit kept me writing. And thanks to Zora Neale Hurston, my spirit grandmother, for shaping who I am.